W8505s

The Secret Life of Hilary Thorne

The Secret Life of Hilary Thorne

Marcia Wood

Atheneum   1988   New York

To Marcia Marshall, who brought life to Hilary,
and to Fred Hecker, who brought life to me.

Grateful acknowledgment is made to Charles Scribner's Sons for permission to make use of the characters from *The Wind in the Willows,* and to Andrea Reynolds for permission to use the Conan Doyle characters Sherlock Holmes and Dr. Watson.

Atheneum
Macmillan Publishing Company
866 Third Avenue, New York, NY 10022
Collier Macmillan Canada, Inc.
Printed in United States of America
First Edition   Designed by Marjorie Zaum
10 9 8 7 6 5 4 3 2 1

Library of Congress Cataloging-in-Publication Data

Wood, Marcia.   The secret life of Hilary Thorne/by Marcia Wood. —1st ed.   p. cm. Bibliography: p. 125 Summary: As Hilary's home life deteriorates after her family's move to the country, her adventures with the book characters she reads about increase to the point where she knows she must learn to control her talents and involve herself more in the real world.   ISBN 0-689-31405-1   [1. Characters and characteristics in literature–Fiction. 2. Moving, Household—Fiction. 3. Space and time—Fiction. 4. Family problems–Fiction.]   I. Title.
        PZ7.W8499Se 1988   [Fic]—dc19 87-30263 CIP AC

The Secret Life
of Hilary Thorne

Chapter One

HILARY SHUT THE BOOK AND ROLLED OVER, CLOS-
ing her eyes against the hot summer sun. She took a
slow, contented breath. The air was sultry, thick,
redolent of both new hay and old times, as if the
world remembered other days like this one. Crickets
hummed in the hedgerows as they had for thousands
of summers past, and the hooves of a horse on a
nearby road played counterpoint to the soft sound
while the bright *toot-toot* of a motorcar horn sang
melody in the distance.

Days like this were meant to be cherished. Lazy
and warm, Hilary slowly made her way over the
fields and down the dusty, hardscrabble road until
she reached the silvery river next to old Toad Hall.

Ratty was on the river in his punt, and when he caught sight of Hilary he began to wave excitedly.

"Hilary, old girl! Where have you been? Positively ages since we've seen you! I've so much—" The end of Ratty's sentence was lost as he struggled to get himself, punt, pole, and picnic basket to the bank without a moment's delay. But haste on a river is tricky, and the faster the rat tried to go, the more tangled up he got, and he ended by upturning everything in the deepest part of the water.

Hilary grinned and sat down on a root to wait for her friend to sort himself out. Ratty finally splashed toward her, and as she lent a hand to help him up the animal continued his chatter.

"Seventeen volumes, all bound in genuine leather," he panted, "despite what Badger said. Of course, he never did understand poetry. And, oh, my dear, you won't believe what Toad is up to now." He tied the line of the punt to a nearby branch.

"What?" asked Hilary obediently.

"Waterskiing. Perfectly ridiculous, at his age." The rat shook his head and shrugged helplessly. "But one never could tell that animal anything. The worst of it is, he's got Mole involved—"

Just then an earsplitting whine ripped the air, and a spangled, very gaudy, green-and-orange speedboat sliced through the river toward them, driving birds, fish, and animals in all directions before it.

4

"In a river, of all places!" Ratty cried, hopping up and down and shaking his fist at the intruder. "Just look at them! Can you believe it?"

At the helm of the boat crouched Mole, clinging desperately to the steering wheel and throwing frantic glances over his shoulder at Toad, who bounced and skittered at the end of the rope that was tied to the stern.

"Toad," the mole cried, "the jump's coming up! I'll try to go around it!"

The toad's reply was choppy but decisive. "No! I want to do it! Go faster! Go faster!" he commanded.

The mole huddled a little closer to the instrument panel, screwed up his eyes and his courage, and pressed the accelerator pedal to the floor.

"No, Toad, no!" yelled Hilary and the rat, alarmed. "Stop!"

With a heart-shaking thump and a long, thin wail, the toad flew up into the air and somersaulted in a nearly perfect circle among the clouds before he landed securely, head first, in the leafy arms of an oak tree some distance from the bank.

A wavering cry came from the plunging boat. "Toad, wait!" called the mole. "I don't know how to turn this thing around!" The mole's words faded away as the speedboat charged headlong down the current.

"If I know that toad, the boat's nearly out of petrol anyway," said the rat, puffing as he and Hilary raced for the big oak. "The question now is, How do we rescue that silly old fool in the tree?"

"I think I can climb up," said Hilary. "But we need some rope."

Rat went in search of rope, and Hilary peered into the tree's green heights. "Toad," she called, "are you hurt?"

"Hilary, child, welcome back," the toad replied weakly. "No, I don't believe so, really. Just—rather—stuck. *Umph!*" The branches of the oak tree shuddered. "Yes," the toad said. "I'm stuck."

Ratty ran up with the rope from the punt. "You silly ass, Toad!" he shouted. "Just what did you hope to accomplish?"

"Don't worry, Toady," Hilary said calmly. "I'm coming up."

She tied the rope securely around her waist and scrambled up the tree until she reached a branch directly under the hapless toad. She took firm hold of his front legs and tugged sharply until the little creature tumbled into her lap.

"Now," she said, unwrapping the rope from around her middle, "since you don't belong to the branch of your family that can climb trees, we're going to hoist you down." She tied one end of the rope around the toad and looped the other end around a sturdy branch before letting it fall to the ground, where Ratty picked it up in a firm grip.

"Now, Toad, when I tell you to, just scoot yourself off the branch. The rope will keep you from falling, and we'll lower you down slowly. But wait till I tell you," said Hilary. The toad nodded.

Hilary scrambled down the tree and took up a position on the rope behind the rat, who, calmer now, said, "What a clever idea, to use the rope. However did you think of it?"

"I read something like it in *Robinson Crusoe*," Hilary replied, then yelled up to the toad, "Okay? Now!"

The toad slid off the branch and dangled and flopped like a fish at the end of his line. "I'm ready!" he called.

Hilary and the rat began to play out their line to bring Toad to the ground, but just before his feet hit bottom, a voice called out from the direction of the Wild Wood.

"Hilary!"

A door slammed.

Startled, Hilary jumped, and her eyes flew open wide.

The country landscape dissolved into the crisp blue-and-white patterns of Hilary's bedroom in the Thornes' new house. Hilary sighed regretfully, rolled herself off the bed, and went downstairs to greet her mother.

Mrs. Thorne hated what she called "grown-up"

clothes and had already shed shoes, suit jacket, and portfolio by the time her daughter got downstairs. Hilary followed the trail of discards into the kitchen and found her mother filling the teakettle.

"Hi, Mom. How'd it go?" Hilary took the kettle from her mother and set it on the stove.

Mrs. Thorne hitched herself up onto the worn wooden countertop and stuck her stockinged legs straight out. "Okay, I guess." She poked her feet in Hilary's direction. "Do they look swollen to you?"

Hilary glanced at her mother's gently waving limbs. "No."

"A miracle that they're not permanently deformed. I'm absolutely certain that high-heeled shoes—"

"—are a conspiracy to cripple the power of women in the workplace," Hilary finished for her. "I know, Mom. Criminal, isn't it?"

Her mother grinned sheepishly. "All right, all right. Just this one time, I'll be quiet." She twisted to reach into the cabinet behind her. "What kind of tea do you want?"

"Let's just have regular." Hilary poured boiling water from the kettle into the teapot, swirled it around for a moment to heat the pot, and dumped it into the sink. She measured loose tea into the warmed pot, poured fresh boiling water over it, and set the teapot and some mugs on a tray.

Mrs. Thorne jumped down from her perch. "Oh, I almost forgot. I got some elephant's ears from that terrific bakery."

She got the bag of flaky cookies from her portfolio and followed her daughter out to the little screened porch that lay beyond the kitchen.

They sat down at the big round table and Hilary poured tea for herself and her mother. Mrs. Thorne stared dreamily into her mug. "Do you think people read tea leaves anymore?" she asked her daughter. "I wonder if I could find someone to teach me how?"

Hilary laughed and shook her head. There was always something her mother wanted to learn. "What did Mr. Thomas say about the sketches?" she asked.

Mrs. Thorne pitched her voice low and drawled, "Super, Carolyn, just fabulous. Super, really. Just one or two minor—very minor—little points."

Hilary laughed, but Mrs. Thorne shook her head. "It's not as funny as it sounds." She took a sip from her mug. "I don't think they really want *new* illustrations for the new edition, just something as close to the old Rackham drawings as possible. They'd use the originals if they could get them. So, since they didn't want me for my own sweet self," Mrs. Thorne struck a tragic pose, "I declined the commission."

"Oh, Mom, that stinks! Your drawings were so much better than Rackham's," Hilary cried. "He made *The Wind in the Willows* seem much too scary. I read it again today, by the way," she added.

"Hilary! Again?" Her mother sounded exasperated. "How many times does that make, now?"

"Eleven."

Mrs. Thorne's earnest brown eyes sought Hilary's clear gray ones. "Hilary," she said, "don't you think you're becoming just a little *too* wrapped up in your books? You're spending an awful lot of time reading—and not much time doing anything else."

"I did a lot of stuff today, Mom," Hilary protested. "I weeded the garden, and I walked all the way into town—"

"To the bookstore?" asked her mother knowingly.

Hilary looked guilty.

"See what I mean?"

Hilary said defensively, "My books are my friends." She took another cookie and dunked it thoroughly in her tea.

Mrs. Thorne sighed and sipped her tea. Presently she said, "How would you like to join the swim club? There's still plenty of the summer left, and it'd be good to make some friends before school starts, wouldn't it?"

"Don't you worry about me, Mom." Hilary patted her mother's hand kindly.

Mrs. Thorne said suddenly, "Hilary, what have you got in your hair?"

Hilary reached up and felt her head. An oak leaf came away in her hand. "Oh, it's just a leaf. I took the woods path into town," she said, and grinned.

Chapter Two

HILARY AND HER MOTHER HAD DINNER ON THE porch. They ate nearly all their meals out there in warm weather; the porch caught every whisper of wind from three directions but was sheltered by screens from the ever-present, ever-hungry New Jersey mosquitoes.

The porch always made Hilary think of her father. The whole house was wonderful—big and old and full of warm wood and smooth edges, with a wide lawn that rolled out to the edge of the woods—but the porch had been one of the things Mr. Thorne had liked most.

"And there's even a porch in back of the kitchen where we can eat in the summertime," he had told them eagerly when he'd discovered the house for sale. "We'll see the sun come up in the morning and watch it set at night—"

He had smiled sheepishly at his own excitement and tried to act more grown-up. "And it's only forty-five minutes from my new office!" But his eyes had sparkled like Christmas lights and he looked just like a kid.

They'd bought the house, of course, and moved in, but Hilary's father had seen very little of the house he'd loved so much.

You're acting like he's dead, Hilary scolded herself. Stop it. He's only busy. The new job that had brought the Thornes to their wonderful house had kept Sam Thorne away from it. He hadn't been home before dark since they'd moved.

Hilary watched fireflies begin their light dance on the lawn. "Mom," she said, "how much longer is Daddy going to have to work such terrible hours?"

"I'm sure it's just the settling-in process," Mrs. Thorne answered cheerfully. "Not only does your father have lots of new responsibilities, remember, but he's come from a small advertising agency, in a town where he knew everyone, to a very big and famous Madison Avenue shop where he's a stranger. It can't be easy."

"Well, no." Hilary moved uncertainly. "It's just that it's all kind of scary. I feel like he's gone away from us, sort of."

"Oh, I don't think so," said her mother comfortingly. She added, "Things would seem less strange to you if you were more occupied. I'm going to join a tap-dancing class next week. Want to come?"

Hilary hunched a shoulder. "I'm not much of a dancer, you know."

"You'd like it if you gave yourself a chance." Mrs. Thorne rose and began to clear the dishes. "Anyway, you'll probably feel better when school starts. You'll have plenty to do then."

"I guess so." Hilary sounded unconvinced.

When headlights finally gleamed through the pines and she heard the distinctive sound of Mr. Thorne's new, racy little car, Hilary dashed through the front door with a whoop and catapulted herself at her father.

"Daddy, you're home," she cried. "Oh, I'm so glad." She grinned suddenly. "You've been so fir away."

It was an old joke between them. Mr. Thorne grinned back. "Don't pine," he answered.

"I'll spruce up, after I balsam," Hilary returned, and they both laughed. Mr. Thorne hugged his daughter.

"You're home earlier tonight," said Hilary eagerly. "Can we read together, or something, for a little while? Like old times?"

"Sure, kiddo," said Mr. Thorne. "Just let me get something to eat and say hi to Mom."

"She's in the basement taking the legs off the Ping-Pong table. She wants to tap dance on it."

Her father rolled his eyes and groaned in exasperation. Hilary just grinned and said, "There's chicken salad in the fridge. I'll pick out a book and meet you in the library."

Hilary thought the library was the best room in the house. Actually, it wasn't a room at all, just a tiny alcove of the living room that the Thornes had partitioned with sliding double doors. There was barely space in it for the old couch and Mr. Thorne's favorite chair, but the windows that looked north and east over the lawn to the tree-covered hills made the room spacious. Gleaming oak bookcases and cabinets stretched from floor to ceiling, and deep red rugs and curtains made the room as warm as though a fire always glowed in the hearth, sheltering the room from storms, both real and imagined, beyond the windowpanes.

Hilary browsed through the bookcases, pulling a volume out here and there and then replacing it, trying to find a book that would be just right for tonight. It was important, tonight, to find a special book, one that would make her dad remember how much fun they always had when they read together. It had been too long since they'd had an evening like this.

Hilary giggled suddenly. What an incredible jumble this library is, she thought. I pity the poor archaeologist who finds this room intact a thousand years from now. What would he make of us?

Books were shelved by whim and latest reading. Not for the Thornes the neat shelves of ordered books alternating with figurines and tasteful conversation pieces. Here, books and more books crammed the shelves. They stood on end; they lay in stacks. Even the space between the top edges of the books and the underside of the next shelf held books, and books and magazines were piled to precarious heights in the corners of the room. Since it was summer, even the fireplace held wicker-handled baskets full of magazines and catalogues.

If you are what you read, mused Hilary, who are we? She picked up a book thoughtfully.

"A pleasant little problem, Watson, don't you agree?" A distinctive voice spoke suddenly. "These library questions are not without interest."

Sherlock Holmes and Dr. Watson materialized next to the bookcases against the far wall. Holmes was comfortable in his dressing gown, and he had his meerschaum pipe in hand. With its stem, he pointed to a certain shelf. "This shelf, for instance. What do you make of it, old boy?"

"Clearly, there are many children in this household," responded Watson readily. The doctor was clad neatly, as befitted a former military man, in the morning clothes customary for gentlemen of the late nineteenth century. His clothing and his face contrasted strongly with Holmes's; for while the great detective's face was sharply angled and planed and wore an expression of intensity, Watson looked open and friendly and kind.

"That is apparent from the number of children's books on these shelves," continued Watson, "but the children are young and cannot read to themselves; thus, we see clean and new-looking books."

Holmes nodded encouragingly, and Watson went on. "I can tell from the extent and the condition of this collection of books that these children are lucky enough to have a mother who is both conscientious and well educated, and a father who can afford to buy such things," he finished triumphantly.

"Watson," Holmes replied warmly, "your detective skills have improved considerably."

"Then I was right?" Watson puffed up in pride.

"Only insofar as you realized that the lady of the house is well educated," Holmes replied. "You didn't notice that these juvenile volumes, different in other ways, all bear the name of Carolyn Thorne as illustrator, and since they are obviously kept carefully together and are rarely disturbed on that rather inconvenient shelf, Carolyn Thorne herself probably owns these books and therefore lives in this house."

Watson's face fell.

"Moreover, there is much else to be learned of Carolyn Thorne from this room," continued Holmes. "She is a woman of wide interests and great—though fleeting—enthusiasms. She acts silly sometimes, probably to offset the formidable intelligence that her library shows. But she is a sensible and practical mother, and looks upon her young daughter as a companion and an equal."

"Your brilliance astonishes me, Holmes," Watson cried.

"Not at all, Watson," replied Holmes. "I simply followed the principals of deduction. Take note, if you will, of the unusually large number of cookbooks that occupy these shelves," he explained. "There are so many—Indian, African, Italian, Japanese, French—but since they are here, and not in the kitchen where they would be easily at hand if wanted, the owner of these books would seem to be quickly interested and easily distracted. Yet anyone with a short attention span would not have studied tropical botany with the books on this shelf here," he gestured, "and Mrs. Thorne did, as her illustrations for this volume prove."

Holmes took *The Jungle Book* from the shelf and began to thumb through it.

Watson had been exploring the shelves as his friend spoke, and now said, "But, Holmes, I see no books on child rearing. How did you determine her views on that?"

"Do you remember the curious incident of the dog that barked in the night? This is the same sort of situation: The fact that there are no such books suggests that this woman knows her own mind on the subject and has no need of fashionable theories."

Holmes continued his study of the shelves and presently remarked, "Mr. Thorne feels somewhat uncomfortable in his new position at the advertising agency, I see."

"Oh, I say, Holmes," said Watson awkwardly. His Victorian sense of propriety was shocked at the reference to a stranger's emotional state.

Holmes brushed off the reproof. "Nonsense, Watson. Look here. This is a man who has worked hard to surround himself with serenity. He's a fly fisherman and an amateur naturalist. Look at the photographs on his desk, in handmade frames. He cherishes his family, his books, and his home. The texture of his life is philosophical and inquisitive. But here," he pointed, "there's a fine film of dust on the desk, and this pipe hasn't been used for days. And in the center of the desk, a stack of volumes that all have the same subject. *What Harvard Business School Never Taught You. In Search of Excellence.* And four, no, five others about becoming a successful businessman. But what does that have to do with his interest in John Muir and Henry David Thoreau and these other naturalists? These books on the desk simply don't fit in with the others in this room."

Holmes turned to the other man. "You remember that these people did not need books to raise their child? The fact that these books are here indicates that Thorne is groping for a way to cope with new responsibilities."

He walked over to another bookcase and picked up a stack of books that had been wedged above the books already on the shelf. "These books, Mrs. Thorne's, were put on a shelf fully six inches below the eye level of an average woman. Since people shelving objects generally put them at eye level, Mrs. Thorne must be shorter than average."

Watson laughed. "It is not often that I find you in error, my friend," he said gleefully, "but I believe you've forgotten something this time. There is a daughter in the house! She probably shelved the books."

"My dear Watson," Holmes replied with a twinkle, "young people of that age do not put things on shelves." He tamped the tobacco in the bowl of his pipe and drew upon it.

Nettled, Watson replied, "And how do you know the age of the child?"

"If I'm not very much mistaken," said Holmes, "she is seated right behind you."

Watson whirled, tried to recover his aplomb, and bowed to Hilary as he said, "My apologies, miss. I had not realized—"

"That's all right, Dr. Watson," replied Hilary, extending her hand. "I had fun, just listening. Did you know that there are actually clubs that get together just to hear about you and Mr. Holmes?"

Watson shook Hilary's hand and made modest sounds in his throat. Hilary could tell he was flattered, though. She went on. "Your stories are terrific, and even famous people join those clubs. Franklin Delano Roosevelt belonged to the Baker Street Irregulars," she said.

Watson looked puzzled. "Roosevelt? I'm afraid—" he started, but Holmes cut in.

"Roosevelt was thirty-second president of the United States of America. He held the office from 1933 to 1945," he said, looking up from the book—volume 26 of the *Encyclopaedia Britannica*—in his hands. "Miss Thorne, I appreciate the opportunity to glimpse the progress of the world since I've known it."

"You're welcome, sir," Hilary said politely. "Is there anything else you'd like to know?"

Watson cleared his throat. "Medical advances," he said. "What has come about?"

"Well," said Hilary thoughtfully, "probably the biggest event in medicine since your time has been the discovery of penicillin. They used to call it the 'miracle drug.' The people who discovered it and identified it won the Nobel Prize. My mom illustrated a story about them."

"Mmm, yes," said Watson abstractedly. "This penicillin. Does it cure consumption?"

Hilary suddenly remembered. "Your wife died of consumption, didn't she?" she asked.

Watson nodded, and Hilary said, "I think consumption is what we call tuberculosis now. I'm not sure if it's penicillin they used to treat it, but hardly anybody gets it anymore."

Watson turned away. "Thank God," he said quietly.

"Other problems are bigger than they used to be, though," said Hilary, chatting on mainly to give Dr. Watson time to recover from such an unusual outburst of emotion. "Some of the drugs have done more harm than good. There were opium dens in your time, weren't there? Now there's drug abuse all over the place, by all kinds of people. Even kids."

Holmes looked intently at Hilary. "Say that again!" he commanded.

Hilary was bewildered. "What? Even kids?"

Holmes began to untie the cord of his dressing gown and turned to Watson. "I never dreamed of anything so diabolical as to permit these things to fall into the hands of children! That's it, man! That's the key to the Westover case! Quickly, we must be off! The game's afoot!"

The library doors slid apart as Sherlock Holmes and Dr. Watson faded into the woodwork, and Mr. Thorne appeared, balancing a tray of milk, cookies, and sandwiches. He put the tray on the coffee table and sank gratefully into his chair.

He grimaced. "It's awfully stuffy in here, Hilary. Haven't you opened any windows? I can still smell my last pipe!"

Hilary went to the window and threw it open. She needed a diversion quickly and glanced at the book in her hand. "How about *A Study in Scarlet*?" she asked.

"Fine," said her father. He rubbed a hand across his forehead and slid down in his chair, shifting his weight impatiently. "Drat this chair," he said irritably. "I think it's outlived its usefulness."

"But, Dad," protested Hilary, "that's Mount Ever-rest. You said you'd never let it go!"

Her father smiled slightly. "Well, it's about time for Mount Ever-rest to be something elegant in leather," he said. "Vice presidents never have looked good in faded chintz."

"Oh, Daddy," said Hilary sadly. She stroked the arm of the old chair affectionately. "This one has been such a friend."

Mr. Thorne looked quizzically at his daughter. "Hilary, why the fuss over a chair?"

"You used to fuss over this chair, too," said Hilary softly.

Her father stretched out an arm to gather Hilary close. His woolen shirt, warm against the cooling night, felt rough against Hilary's cheek, but it smelled fresh and faintly piny. Its scent reminded Hilary of their fishing trip to Yellowstone last year. She hugged her father.

"Is it too lonely for you here?" he asked. "I know you're not used to all this—this space and quiet."

"Oh, no, Daddy, I love it," she assured him. "I like the privacy of the woods. I guess you could say I'm re-leaved."

Mr. Thorne smiled but said, "Relieved? That's a funny word to use. What do you mean?"

Hilary thought a moment, trying to analyze her feelings. She'd never worked it out in words before. "Well," she started slowly, "before, in town, I used to like to watch other people. I'd make up stories about who they were and what they were doing—you know?"

Her father nodded.

She went on. "Well, one day I realized if I could invent all that stuff about them, they could invent stuff about me, too. And that made me really nervous. Even when I knew in my head that what I was

24

doing was okay, I could always imagine that it would seem wrong to someone else."

She laughed a little to herself. "One time," she said, "my school had a vacation day when the public schools didn't, and I was afraid to go outside because I thought a truant officer would come and scoop me up because I wasn't in school."

"But that town didn't even have truant officers," said her father.

"Well, I didn't know that," she said. "There are always truant officers in books. But here I don't have to worry about what other people think. I can relax, at least until school starts."

Mr. Thorne smiled, but his eyes were serious. "I wonder if we've made a mistake, raising you the way we have."

Hilary was puzzled. "What do you mean?"

"Well, I hate to see you so uncomfortable around other people," he replied. "Maybe Mom and I should have spent less time reading and fishing and doing the things we liked with you and more time making sure you have the skills you need to get along in the world."

That made Hilary sit up straight. "But, Dad," she said in surprise, "you always say that there isn't a better way to learn about the world than fishing! You said that challenging nature was the best way to learn to understand it!"

"And I still believe that," replied her father. "But maybe 'nature' and 'the world' aren't necessarily interchangeable terms. I'm beginning to wonder. None of the rules I know seem to apply anymore. In New York—" His voice trailed off and his thoughts took their own course. His face deepened with care.

"Daddy?" Hilary said softly.

Mr. Thorne recalled himself with an effort. "Sorry, kiddo." He smiled slightly. "The point I'm trying to make is that you should feel all right, not all wrong, wherever you are. You need to get out more, build your self-confidence, make friends. You should be putting together your own world, not living in your mother's and mine."

Actually, Hilary reflected, she did have a world of her own.

Hilary had never told her parents about her discovery, about how she'd learned to bring the characters in her books to life. She'd found out about the trick by accident when she was six years old, almost as soon as she learned to read.

It had been a snowy day. School had been closed, and Mommy was busy. "Read a book," she'd said to Hilary.

"A whole book by myself?" So far, Hilary had only read books a page at a time, slowly and painstakingly, and only when it was her turn to read out loud in class. At home, her parents always read to her.

"Try," said her mother absently, chewing on the tip of a paintbrush.

"But what book?" asked Hilary blankly.

"I don't know," said her mother, leaning into her canvas. "Whatever suits your fancy."

Fancy. Hilary went downstairs to look for a fancy book.

And she found one, its binding scrolled and gilded and its pages deckle-edged. It smelled fancy, too, like candles and perfume and the church on Christmas Eve. What kind of a book was this? The letters on the cover were so elaborate that Hilary could barely make them out—*Song* something—but the book was small, almost as small as her hand. Something so little must be meant for little people. She opened the book.

A flower fell out. A flat flower, a fragile, tissue-thin flower, but a flower all the same, a pink rose. Hilary lifted it in both hands, carefully. She thought she could just catch an echo of its soft, old scent.

She stared at the book in awe. It must be magic to make flowers, she thought, and in wintertime too. A magic book. Holding her breath in excitement, she turned to the first page.

The words inside were easier to read than the ones on the cover, and they were put down in short lines. Hilary liked that. She sounded the words out carefully:

Merrily, merrily shall I live now,
Under the blossom that hangs on the bough.

"Hello, there," said a voice at her side. "I'm Ariel. Do you like to play games?" And suddenly Hilary wasn't lonely anymore.

That was the first time. At first, it had been hard—she had to sound out the words and then shut her eyes tight and *concentrate*. But it got easier. All she had to do now was pick up a book and she was gone. Magic.

She'd been all over the world by this time, and in all the ages of history: She'd been to Boston during the Revolutionary War with Johnny Tremain; she'd been to Paris, India, and the Island of the Blue Dolphins; she'd even written a play with Jo March and narrowly escaped IT with Charles Wallace and Meg Murry. (She still felt breathless when she thought about *A Wrinkle in Time*.)

Besides, how would she explain it, she wondered now for what must have been the ten thousandth time at least. Gee, Mom, the characters in my books really come to life for me. Hey, Dad, guess what? I can go wherever my books will take me!

Would they believe it was magic? Even her parents, as wonderful as they were, would probably have some trouble with that. If they thought even for a split second that I really believed I was magic, she thought, they'd think I'd lost it for sure, and then they'd feel obligated to do something responsible.

That's always what happened in books.

They might take her to a child psychologist, like in *Harriet the Spy*. Or maybe boarding school even, like in *Jane Eyre*. She shivered.

Better not to risk it.

Much better to keep quiet, she thought, and make Mom and Dad happy.

Hilary turned a dazzling smile on her father. "I'll try to be more outgoing when school starts," she promised.

"Thanks, kiddo." Her father tousled her hair. "Just don't go too far out, please."

Hilary laughed but thought, What fun. "Daddy, is your new job really terrible?" she asked abruptly. "How come you're never home anymore?"

Mr. Thorne sat up in his chair in surprise, and the old chair's springs creaked in protest. "Why, no, it's not terrible at all," he said. "This job is the best thing that ever happened to us. Kiddo, for the very first time in our lives almost anything that you or Mom could want, I can give you. That's not terrible, not by a long shot," he said with pride. "It's worth a little extra time."

Hilary was overwhelmed with love for her brave

and generous father. He gave them so much. She wanted to give him something, to share something special of her own that would show him how she felt. "Hey, Dad, you know what?"

But the phone rang. Mr. Thorne picked it up.

It was as though a light bulb had popped and left the room dark and bitter smelling. Her father's face went tight and tired as he listened on the phone. When he talked into the receiver, he actually shouted once or twice, and Hilary watched curiously. That wasn't like him at all—why was he yelling?

When he hung up her father said, "I've got to get to the office."

"Now?" said Hilary.

"There's an emergency with a big client's commercial," said her father shortly. He was already out of his chair and at the desk, picking up his briefcase and his keys.

Hilary tried to hold on to her father. "But, Daddy, you promised."

"Kiddo, I'm sorry. There's nothing I can do."

Hilary was hurt. He'd never broken a promise to her before. And here she'd been all ready to let him know her secret.

Mr. Thorne watched his daughter's face and looked even more unhappy. He took a step back toward Hilary. "Tell you what," he said uncertainly. "I'll bring you home a tape or something."

"I don't want a tape or something," Hilary said petulantly. "I don't want anything."

Mr. Thorne flashed anger suddenly. "Well, then you won't get anything."

He'd never raised his voice to her before. Something had happened here, something had changed, but before Hilary could figure out what it was, her father was gone.

Chapter Three

IN AUTUMN, THE ROLLING HILLS BEHIND THE Thorne house dropped their demure cloaks of green and arrayed themselves in brazen color; even the air took on a provocative, sharp edge that reminded Hilary of the first bite of a new apple, firm and crackling and cool. The snap and color were invigorating after the long, lethargic summer, and everyone in the house was stirred to action: Hilary started school, Mrs. Thorne began a new series of illustrations and six new classes, and Mr. Thorne worked ever-longer hours at his office in the city.

Hilary walked home from school along the paths that laced the hills behind the house. Occasionally a deer in a darkened, winter-ready coat sprang, alarmed, from a thicket, but today Hilary took little joy from her surroundings. She kicked at a stone, and sighed.

I don't know what Daddy's going to say, she thought. Then she thought, Does it matter? I won't hear him say it. I never see him anymore.

She sighed again. Trouble. Toil and trouble. That witch.

Mrs. Kane, the English teacher, was the source of the immediate problem. Last week, she'd kept Hilary after class—already, and they hadn't even been in school a month.

"Hilary." Mrs. Kane was a no-nonsense sort of woman, feared and respected in equal measures by her students. It was rumored that some kids in the higher grades actually liked Mrs. Kane, but Hilary found that hard to believe.

"Hilary," Mrs. Kane repeated, "I must tell you that I am very disappointed in your work to date." The teacher's long, thin fingers turned over some papers on the desk and tapped, quietly, ominously, against one of them. "Your records show you to be exceptionally intelligent, exceptionally imaginative, but I have yet to observe any indication of either firsthand."

Hilary cast around in her mind for a reply, but her exceptional imagination failed her. She kept her eyes fixed on the near corner of Mrs. Kane's desk.

"You haven't turned in a homework assignment since the second day of term," Mrs. Kane continued. "Will you tell me why?"

Hilary was appalled. All this fuss for a few crummy vocabulary lists? Yes, I can tell you why, you pompous old bat, Hilary shot back at her mentally. Because I've never seen anything so stupid as your boring lists of words. I can spend my time better with books.

Hilary had been reading a lot lately.

She let her eyes stray briefly to Mrs. Kane's face, then dropped them. Mrs. Kane, if given the chance, would probably be able to read the mutiny mirrored there.

"Can you tell me why?" Variations on a theme.

Hilary shook her head.

"Will you tell me why you never participate in class discussions?"

Hilary kept her head bowed and her face hidden behind a curtain of hair.

"These questions are not rhetorical, Hilary," Mrs. Kane said dryly.

Hilary grinned and dared a glance at the teacher's face.

Mrs. Kane saw it. She made a sudden change in strategy. "Hilary, what do you do when you go home in the afternoon?" she asked.

Hilary was startled. "I read," she said.

"Read? Read what?" asked the teacher sharply.

Hilary lifted a hand, shrugged.

"I'm sorry. Poor question." Mrs. Kane rephrased it. "I should have said, What are you reading now?"

"*The Age of Chivalry,*" Hilary replied warily.

"Ah, yes, by Thomas Bulfinch." Mrs. Kane was pleased. "Like it?"

"Yes. I've read it before," Hilary said.

"A re-reader. Good." Mrs. Kane approved. "To paraphrase Thomas Carlyle, books are friends that will never fail you."

She came around the side of the desk and sat on the corner nearest Hilary so that the girl's gaze was forced upward. Hilary noticed that the teacher's eyes were a lovely rich brown behind the thick eyeglasses. And she thought of books as friends, too. Hilary warmed a little toward the teacher.

"Now, tell me," said Mrs. Kane, almost as if she cared about the answer, Hilary thought, "what book have you chosen to read for your term report?"

"*Mythology,*" Hilary replied.

"By Edith Hamilton? Ambitious of you," said Mrs. Kane. "Well, small wonder you don't care for vocabulary lists. Not quite on the same scale as Greek gods and knights in shining armor, are they?"

The teacher tapped a pencil purposefully on the edge of the desk, her head bent in thought. She returned to her chair, took the pencil in both hands, and regarded Hilary over it.

"Hilary, I'll make you a deal. I'll excuse you from vocabulary assignments,"—she held up a hand to check Hilary's response—"but only if you'll do another kind of homework. You may turn in book reports instead of word lists. One for one. Agreed?"

Hilary agreed excitedly. Mrs. Kane actually seems to like me, she thought. Maybe I'm not as strange as I thought I was. "I'll do it!"

"Thank you," said Mrs. Kane dryly.

Hilary rushed home and got to work. She decided to do her first report on *From the Mixed-up Files of Mrs. Basil E. Frankweiler.* That had been fun—especially the part in the fountain. Hilary worked hard and she turned in her report proudly the next day. She'd done a good job, she was sure.

Hilary scowled, jammed her hands more deeply in her pockets, and spun another innocent stone into oblivion as she remembered the conversation. You just can't trust anyone, she muttered darkly to herself.

The report, handed in so eagerly, so proudly, last week had been returned. It hung like a weight in her backpack and her conscience. *D.*

Hilary had never before in her life received a *D.* And the comment—oh, it was all so humiliating. She probed the remembrance gingerly but persistently, as if it were an aching tooth.

"I expected more from you, Hilary. Mrs. Frankweiler *is* a fun book to read," Mrs. Kane had written. "But there's more to it than adventure. How were Claudia and Jamie affected by their experiences? What is the author trying to communicate? Do you agree with what she has to say? Don't take what you read so literally. *Think* about it."

I should have done those stupid vocabulary lists, Hilary reflected, and been just like everyone else. She slammed the kitchen door. It doesn't pay to be different. Nobody cares about me.

Mrs. Thorne's voice floated down the stairs from her studio. "Hilary, is that you?" she called.

"Yes!" Hilary snapped. "Who did you think?"

"Come see!"

Hilary sighed, threw her backpack in a corner of the kitchen, and stomped up the stairs to the skylit studio.

When she got there she almost forgot she was angry. Twelve completed illustrations for a collection of poetry hung evenly along the walls of the studio. All the canvases were the same size; they looked like windows, windows that each opened onto very different views.

"Guess which is which!" Mrs. Thorne bubbled with excitement. She pushed her daughter to the nearest one. "No, wait. Start over there," she said, and turned Hilary around.

"Hold on, Mom," Hilary said, laughing a little. "Does it matter where I start? Light somewhere, would you please? You're making me dizzy."

Mrs. Thorne settled on a stool. "Sorry, kiddo," she said. "I guess I always get a little silly whenever I've finished a project. I'll behave," she promised. "Start there." She pointed.

The scene was a muted one, a colonial village at night. The viewer stood at the top of the high street and saw the village ramble down a gentle hill to meet the wharf, and a larger town on the opposite shore of a moonlit bay. Alone among the buildings in the town a church tower was lit, with a pair of lanterns that cast thin but steady beams. At the bottom of the village street, a horse's hooves and flying tail were barely discernible in the gloom, as horse and rider rounded a corner at speed.

" 'A shape in the moonlight, a bulk in the dark, And beneath, from the pebbles, in passing, a spark,' " quoted Hilary. "Mom, that's great. Mostly in pictures you see Paul Revere on a galloping horse with his cloak flapping in the breeze, but here, you only get a hint of what's going on, so you want to get around that corner and find out the rest. Mom, it's wonderful," she said. "It really is."

In the next painting, a man stood pensively by a

small-paned window, looking out at something beyond the range of the viewer's eye. The man was
tired, his shoulders slumped. Behind him was a desk,
stacked with papers that spilled from neat piles. To
one side was a bookcase filled with endless rows of
identical, thick ledgers. One of the ledgers was missing from the ranks, and it lay open on the desk. A
wastebasket was tipped over on the floor, as though
it had been kicked, and there was a broken pencil
beneath the chair.

The man's face held an expression of yearning as
he looked beyond the room through the window.

"That's Daddy!" cried Hilary, shocked.

"Yes," agreed her mother. " 'Sea Fever' did re-
mind me of him. Don't you think he's been acting
lately like he's caged?"

What shocked Hilary about the picture was the
idea, new to her, that her father had problems—
dark, frightening, mysterious problems she knew
nothing about—and the thought scared her, scared
her all the way down to the bedrock of her soul.

She wheeled on her mother. "How could you
put Daddy in a picture like that?" she demanded
angrily.

"Sweetie, what's wrong with that?" Mrs.
Thorne's voice was light. "I've used you both as mod-
els before."

"But you've only put the good stuff in before—

not like this! This is—this is an invasion!" Hilary cried. "What are people going to think about us?"

"Hilary, this isn't an invasion. People aren't going to intrude on our family because a figure in my painting looks like my husband—I doubt that anyone will even notice," said Mrs. Thorne calmly.

But Hilary stormed on. "How can you make Daddy look like that? How can you do that?" Tears streaked her face. "You've betrayed us!"

"Oh, no, Hilary." Mrs. Thorne stretched out a hand to her daughter, but Hilary struck it away.

"Get away from me, just get away. You just wait until Daddy gets home. He'll make you stop. You're going to have to do your stupid painting all over again."

Hilary whirled, seized her mother's jar of brush cleaner, hurled it at the painting, and bolted from the room.

Hilary didn't know her father had come home until he was at the door of her room.

"Daddy, oh, I'm so glad you're finally here," Hilary cried, but her advance was rebuffed by an iron arm.

"What the hell is going on here, Hilary?" snapped Mr. Thorne in a voice that Hilary had never heard before. "The last thing I need is to come home to this!"

"Daddy, wait," pleaded Hilary. "You don't understand—"

"There's nothing to understand," shouted this strange, new father of hers. "What kind of person are you? How dare you destroy another person's property?"

He glared at Hilary, who stood small and silent in the center of the room, and continued in a cold, a very cold voice, "Stay up here tonight. I don't want to have to deal with you. All I want is peace."

"Daddy, wait! Please!"

He shut the door behind him.

For a long time, Hilary did nothing except to stand perfectly still in the middle of the room, her hands at her sides, her eyes focused carefully on the bright curtains at the window. What a sharp edge there is between the blue and the white, she thought. Ugly. Things shouldn't be so hard.

Finally, she sat down on the bed and leaned her head against the bedpost. I can't stay here anymore, she thought. I can't. She reached almost desperately for her book. Maybe Merlin can help me. Maybe he'll change me into—into a tree, she thought. It's too hard to be a person.

Chapter Four

THE MOON WAS A SMILE OF PROMISE IN THE SPRING
night sky, but in front of Hilary spread the forest of
Brécéliande, a dark, mysterious place that buried the
hope of the moon beneath a tangle of leaves and
branches. From deep inside the forest came the
disembodied noises of the night: the haunting call of
the whippoorwill and the answer of its mate, a rustle
of underbrush quickly silenced, a sudden angry
screech from a small animal. Cool, damp air hung
around the forest like a shroud.

Hilary shivered.

Then a branch snapped behind her and Hilary
spun around. She crouched instinctively toward the
ground as she did so, poised for flight like the rabbit
who fears the fox.

The intruder, though, did not look threatening. He was a boy of about her own age, rather small, with tousled brown hair and wide eyes. He wasn't even dressed in ancient clothing—no hose, no singlet, and not a link of armor. He had on a denim jacket, jeans, and high-topped sneakers. And he looked as startled as Hilary felt. He'd recoiled at the sight of her and was backed against a sapling that bowed under his weight.

Hilary's mouth fell open. She'd never met anyone of her own world in her travels before. "Who are you?" she demanded finally. "How did you get here, and what are you doing?"

When he opened his mouth, however, the boy didn't sound like he came from Hilary's world. "Prithee, fair damsel," he said. "Take not umbrage at my poor presence. It was another such as yourself who caused me thus and it is beyond my power to make amends."

Hilary snickered. However romantic that sort of talk was from a handsome knight dressed in velvets and satin, from a boy who wore a T-shirt that said LIFE'S A BEACH, it was silly. The boy lamented, "Only the black arts and the good Lord know what is this hex upon my chest! Woe, woe, this is a pretty burden for Gawain, knight of the Table Round! My fair Katherine will never look upon a man with these blue leggings! And lookest thou upon my feet!"

It was too much. "If you want me to take you

seriously," Hilary said sternly, "speak normally."

The boy frowned in perplexity. "Do fairies not require formal speech from mortals?" he asked. " 'Twas thus my woes began. I failed to greet Niniane when I passed her on the road—I did not even see her—and, lo, she turned me into a hideous dwarf!"

Hilary stared at him in surprise. "I'm not a fairy, and you're not hideous! Where I come from, you'd look perfectly normal," she said.

Gawain shook his head despairingly. But there was a twinkle deep in the back of his eye, as if he were pretending, as if perhaps his plight amused and did not frighten him. Hilary liked him for that.

"What are you going to do?" she asked.

" 'Tis naught to do," Gawain said. He straightened his shoulders. "I'm pledged to find Merlin for the king, and I must keep my word. The whispers say the wizard Merlin has built a tower in this forest."

"You're going to walk around like that—looking like a hideous dwarf?" asked Hilary, surprised. "What will your people think of you?"

Gawain shrugged. "Merlin won't take fright from a dwarf."

There was, apparently, more to being a knight than riding a white horse. This one was very brave. "Can I come with you?" Hilary asked tentatively. "I need Merlin, too."

Gawain bowed gracefully, despite the clumsy

sneakers on his feet. " 'Twould be a pleasure to me."

They made their way to the edge of the trees and found a narrow path that led, with many bends and turns, deep into the heart of the forest. Soon the light of the moon was far behind them, and they were enveloped by the cold and the dark. Wind cried through the trees with the voice of a sad mandolin. Hilary would have stopped right there and waited for morning, but Gawain pushed ahead.

" 'Tis safer to keep moving," he murmured just above his breath. The forest was large, and they each felt quite small.

Then the underbrush rattled in front of them, and Hilary let out a screech. The noise scuttled away at her cry.

Gawain said reproachfully, "I think they might be more afraid of us than we are of them!"

"Who are 'they'? Lions and tigers and bears?" joked Hilary feebly. "Oh, my!"

"No," said Gawain. "Wild boars, and wolves, and witches. Stay close."

Hilary stayed close.

They walked on through the night, more by touch and by sense than by sight. Gawain called out Merlin's name from time to time, but silence was the answer.

"Why doesn't he answer?" asked Hilary almost petulantly. She was getting tired. "Why won't he come?"

Presently the darkness began to thin. Hilary supposed that, outside the trees, the sun was beginning to rise. They could distinguish movement and see shapes now, when the wind gusted through tree branches and small animals raced across their path, but half-light was more frightening than the dark. Trees, invisible before, now looked like bears or druids, and leafless branches looked like spectral hands.

Gawain attacked a giant snake that turned out to be a vine, and Hilary grumbled, "How are we going to find Merlin in all this confusion? Every time we see something, it turns out to be something else! It's all tricks!"

"When the illusions are not of our imaginings," answered Gawain, "we'll know we're getting close to magic. That will mean Merlin is nigh."

Somehow the idea of becoming a tree had begun to lose its appeal. Trees spent their whole lives in dark forests. "Can't we just rest for a minute?" pleaded Hilary. "We've been walking all night."

"For a minute, then," conceded Gawain. "Over there, by that pile of rocks."

They climbed up among the nubby, scaly rocks and settled in a cleft just under the spiny ridge at the top of the pile. The face of the rocky cliff was mottled with a thick, soft moss that seemed still warm from the sun of the day before. Hilary stretched and felt her muscles relax one by one.

"Look," said Gawain presently, pointing out across the treetops.

At first Hilary didn't see anything. The view through the trees was unrelentingly green.

"There," Gawain said again.

Hilary leaned forward and strained her eyes in the direction of his hand.

"The trees look a little thicker, more shadowy over there," she said doubtfully. "Is that what you mean?"

"Aye," said Gawain.

"What's over there?"

"I do not know," he replied. "Perhaps Merlin's tower, perhaps another pile of rocks." He stood up, balancing easily on the slope of the rock.

"It might be something else," said Hilary pessimistically. "Or it might be nothing." She was so tired and had finally sat down. She didn't want to leave the rock.

Gawain answered spiritedly, "But if we just sit here we shall not find out. Come."

Hilary snuggled deeper into her nest. She pulled the moss, as warm as fur, around herself. "I don't really need to find Merlin right away," she demurred.

"I do," said Gawain. "And 'twould be folly to leave you alone in the forest of Brécéliande. Come." He clambered over the rock face to Hilary and took her hands to pull her up.

Mulishly, Hilary resisted, so Gawain dug his heels into the moss and yanked her.

A roar of anger rolled across the forest, welling up from the rock beneath them. The rock shuddered and cracked and the earth tipped upward. A gigantic head with red and heated eyes reared from beyond the ridge of the rock.

"Hold fast!" cried Gawain.

There wasn't any time for talk. A scaly tail danced over them and swung close. Acrid breath seared their faces and jagged teeth crashed like mighty cymbals above them, as the dragon bucked and twisted to reach the mites that pricked his back. Hilary and Gawain clung grimly, fingers clenched and pulling at the dragon's mossy fur.

They were on the nape of his neck, and neither teeth nor tail could touch them, but if they let go they'd be caught. They were swooped back and forth in bone-jarring jerks and starts. Their ears rang and their stomachs shook loose from their backbones.

If only they'd found Merlin—he could have saved them from this! Hilary thought she couldn't last much longer. Her hands were losing their grip, and she was slipping slowly down the dragon's flank. The dragon's tail flicked her leg.

Gawain saw. He unlaced the fingers of one hand from their hold and reached for Hilary. "Hold onto me!" he yelled.

"No," she cried. "We'll both fall!"

"Hold on!" he insisted. "We will save each other!"

She grabbed onto his wrist, and his fingers curled around hers. With the other hand and with his knees and elbows and his rubber-soled shoes, he inched himself up, up to the dragon's backbone, and he pulled Hilary up behind him. Then he lowered himself over one side of the horny ridge of the dragon's spine and gestured to Hilary to stay where she was.

The thrashing grew chaotic and the roaring in their ears rose to an unbearable pitch. When Gawain yelled, his words were whipped away and Hilary could barely understand him. "He doesn't like us holding on! Let go of his fur and just hold onto my hands!"

Draped over the dragon's back like saddlebags on a mule, they clasped hands. Gawain had them balanced perfectly; the weight of one kept the other from sliding down. Slowly, since they weren't pulling on his fur anymore, the dragon's ire subsided. The wild ride ended. The dragon snorted once or twice and settled himself back into his nap.

When everything was quiet, Hilary and Gawain unclasped their hands and slid lightly down the scaly back. They ran together toward the thickness of the trees.

They stopped some distance from the dragon's

nest and inhaled the fresh forest air. Hilary's heart-
beat slowed its frantic tempo. When they had caught
their breaths, Gawain grinned crookedly and said,
"Now, where are we?"

"Now. Now." The words piped among the leaves
and echoed in bass tones against the cliffs. Vines quiv-
ered in unison; the sound in the forest swelled on a
common note like an orchestra in tune. The note
held, the forest stilled expectantly, and slowly, round
and sonorous, a single voice wove toward them.

"I am here."

"Merlin?" said Gawain.

"Now and forever." The forest sighed in sympathy.

"We can't see you," said Hilary.

"It is not to be." The voice was sad.

"Didn't you see us with the dragon?" asked Hilary in surprise. "Why didn't you help us?"

"Did I not?" The voice deepened.

"Gawain saved me," said Hilary.

"We saved each other," corrected Gawain.

"It is one."

Hilary wasn't quite sure what he meant. Silence
beat, and then Gawain said, "The king bade me es-
cort you back to Castle Carduel."

Merlin's voice softened. "It is not to be."

"He wants you," said Gawain. "I cannot return
without you."

"You must. You are necessary." The voice was fainter. "To the pretty Katherine as well as to your liege."

"But what will I tell him?"

They could hardly hear Merlin now. The voice was soft, and dying. "Tell him, knight, to bring the Grail to Carduel, and for your pains the spell of Niniane will break. No man will ever see me more, except in deeds."

"What is the Grail?" asked Gawain. "What is that?"

"In deeds?" asked Hilary. "What does that mean?"

But the only answer was the whisper of the wind.

Chapter Five

AFTER A SILENT DINNER, HILARY CREPT UP TO HER mother's studio to apologize. Both her mother and her father were there, and she paused outside the doorway in the shadows of the staircase. To face her father at the moment was more than she could bear.

The studio was brightly lit against the October night that pressed in at the uncurtained windows. Mr. Thorne stood with his back to the room and looked out toward hills obscured by darkness.

Mrs. Thorne was cleaning her materials. "Well, the painting will be all right," she said calmly, "but I'm not so sure about Hilary."

Mr. Thorne did not reply.

"You were a little hard on her," Mrs. Thorne said gently.

Hilary nodded vigorously in the shadows.

"I suppose so," said Mr. Thorne reluctantly.

Carolyn Thorne put down her tools and crossed the room to stand behind her husband. She folded her arms around him and laid her head upon his shoulder. "What's wrong, Sam?"

He shrugged.

"You've acted angry and unhappy ever since we came here," Mrs. Thorne said.

Sam Thorne made an impatient gesture. "Unhappy?" he repeated. "What on earth have I got to be unhappy about? We have everything we ever wanted—a big house in the country, money for all the classes you want, new cars. Isn't that enough to make *you* happy?"

Mrs. Thorne was silent for a moment. "Sam," she said at last, "I do appreciate everything you've done for us. It's just that—is it worth the price?"

Mr. Thorne sighed and said with exaggerated patience, "I'm tired, Carolyn, that's all." He paused, then added somewhat nastily, "I'm giving you a good life."

"Sam, that's not fair," said Mrs. Thorne sharply. "You don't *give* me a life; we make our lives together."

Mr. Thorne flung away. "Forget it, Carolyn, just forget it." He went to the door. "I've got work to do."

Hilary sped silently to her room.

Mrs. Thorne followed her husband to the head

of the staircase and raised her voice behind him. "Sam, I never asked you for any of this. You didn't have to buy me, you know."

Mr. Thorne snapped, "Carolyn, I told you to forget it." He didn't even pause on his way down the stairs.

Mrs. Thorne flew back into her studio and slammed the door.

An echoing slam came from the library. The old house trembled.

Hilary closed the door of her room soundlessly. We all need help, she thought. Each other's help, came a thought out of nowhere.

But this isn't like Gawain and the dragon, she argued with herself. What can I do?

She sighed and reached for her mythology book. A book report was due on Monday.

The cliff reared high above the water's edge; it made Hilary dizzy to look down, so she looked outward instead, toward the harbor's mouth. The sea was peppered with the red square sails of fishing boats; their color and the blue sky and ocher rocks around the sea made a brilliant picture. Shapes were sharp in this shadowless land; the world was young and unworn.

A white figure moved steadily along the ridge, and Hilary watched idly as it came closer. Presently the figure became a girl in a short, belted tunic, who covered the ground with long and rhythmic strides. She flashed a grin at Hilary as she came near and slowed to a stop beside her.

"Running away?" asked Hilary, as the girl caught her breath, "or just running?"

The girl smiled. "A bit of both, I think." She was lithe and fair, with blond hair in braids around her head and eyes that struck sparks when she laughed. "I run so that I may escape the fate of marriage." She dropped down beside Hilary and stretched full-length on the warm rock.

"Oh, I know about you," cried Hilary. "You're Atalanta! You're the one who won't marry anyone who can't beat you in a footrace!"

"And by the grace of Hermes and Athena, no one has." Atalanta touched her forehead with a finger in a gesture of thanks to the gods. "News travels, does it not? How people gossip!" Atalanta shook her head ruefully.

"Well, gee," said Hilary, "if you're as great an athlete as they say you are, no wonder you don't want to be tied to a house. Did you really sail with Jason and the Argonauts? And kill the Calydonian boar?"

"Yes." Atalanta picked up a handful of sand from the rock and let it trickle slowly through her fingers. "My father is ashamed of my unfeminine behavior—until I do something no *man* can. Then he is proud enough to forget I am a girl."

Hilary agreed. "My mother says, if a woman wants a man's job, she has to be able to do it better than a man ever could. Otherwise, no one takes her seriously."

"So," said Atalanta, "it is good that we can."

Hilary grinned and asked, "Who are you racing this time?"

"Milanion," Atalanta answered. "I know him not. Many come just for the challenge—not because they care for *me.*"

"But what would you do if one of them won?"

"One will not." Atalanta was confident. "I do all the things I must to win. I make propitiation to the gods, and, of course, I keep myself prepared." She cocked her head at Hilary. "Would you like to help?"

"Sure," Hilary said right away. "What can I do?"

"Run with me," said Atalanta, rising to her feet. "It is more fun in company."

Hilary liked to run, which was fortunate because during the next three days she and Atalanta ran every kilometer of the Arcadian countryside. They ran through settlements built with bricks of baked clay, past encampments of soldiers dressed in cuirasses and greaves, along cliffs where the Mediterranean thundered against the rocks. Hilary could barely keep the pace, but Atalanta could even talk as she ran.

Atalanta talked quite a lot, and she was very confident that what she had to say was of interest to her listener. Hilary learned more about the Greek city-states than she ever wanted to know.

Once, just to stem the tide, Hilary asked, "But why is it that you don't want to get married?"

Atalanta stared at her. "And live my life in the shadow of somebody else?"

Hilary nodded in agreement. Atalanta would find it hard to be subdued.

On race day the sun was brazen in the sky, but a breeze came in from the sea and made the air cool. Anticipation of the contest made Atalanta restless.

"There is no need to wait for sundown to begin the race," she said. "The wind is cool enough today. Hilary, will you tell Milanion?"

Hilary walked over to the guest house where Milanion was quartered. A slight, dark-haired man came outside in answer to her call and raised his eyebrows questioningly.

"You called for me?" He had a toneless voice. His eyes were hard.

Hilary relayed Atalanta's message.

"It makes no difference to me," said Milanion carelessly. "The sooner I return to Athens the better pleased I will be."

He seemed so cold. Not very loverlike at all. Hilary asked impulsively, "Why do you want to marry Atalanta?"

"I am interested in winning, not wedding," replied Milanion. "This woman cannot be allowed to triumph over men the way she does. She must be shown her place, and I will do it."

Hilary reported back to Atalanta and shivered. "Be careful," she begged the other girl. "There's something scary about him."

Atalanta laughed. "Do not worry. I am the best at what I do. I will not lose."

The course looped amid outcroppings of rock and silver groves of olive trees not far away from town. A crowd of spectators gathered at the starting line. Atalanta joked with many of them as she waited for the start. Milanion spoke to no one.

Then the white flag dropped.

Atalanta started out with easy strides and quickly outdistanced Milanion. She reached the first turn of the course and rounded it well ahead of her opponent.

Everyone cheered.

Then Milanion reached into the folds of his tunic and brought out something that he tossed in Atalanta's path.

Atalanta scarcely broke stride as she scooped up the object, then grinned and waved it at Hilary.

Hilary jogged out to the track and kept pace beside Atalanta. "What are you doing? Keep your mind on the race, for Pete's sake!"

"But look! Never have I seen the like of this before!" Atalanta held out the object.

It was an apple—a beautiful, perfect apple molded from solid, stunning gold, shining and irresistible.

Suddenly Hilary realized that it was possible to cheat in a foot race.

"Atalanta," she said urgently, "don't get distracted. You're out here to race, remember?"

Atalanta said, "Oh, I have plenty of time!"

"Be careful," begged Hilary.

Atalanta laughed and waved Hilary away.

Milanion threw out another golden apple. This time the apple rolled behind Atalanta and she turned back to get it.

Milanion gained ground.

"Atalanta!" Hilary yelled. "Pay attention!"

The third golden apple rolled off the track and nestled deeply among the daisies that studded the hillside and shone no less brightly than the gold.

Atalanta hesitated, but Milanion seemed well behind. She stepped lightly off the track and bent to hunt for the apple. But it hadn't landed near the road, and her search took her far, then farther from the track.

Milanion passed her and crossed the finish line.

A roar of surprise came from the crowd. Atalanta looked up, uncomprehending.

Milanion walked back to her. "My contest, I believe," he said coolly.

Atalanta bowed with the dignity of a sportsman, but there was despair in her eyes. "May I continue to live here in Arcadia?" she asked.

Milanion shook his head. "We are going to live in Athens."

Hilary could hardly believe it, but it all fit together.

Daddy's just like Atalanta, she thought breathlessly. He was going along doing what he liked to do, living the way he liked to, and then these people with the new job came along and tempted him with a lot of money, like Milanion got Atalanta to Athens by tempting her with golden apples. Daddy got distracted from his path, too, so now he's stuck.

She could hardly wait to tell him what she'd learned. She dashed down the stairs and hurled herself through the library doors. "Daddy," she said eagerly, "can't you see what this new job of yours is doing? It's distracting you from what you really care about!"

"Not now, Hilary," said her father expressionlessly. He didn't even look up from his work.

But Hilary rushed on. "You're hardly ever home, you never have time to walk in the woods or go fishing or take canoe trips like we used to, and when you are home you either get mad and yell or you shut yourself up in here for hours at a time. And I'll tell you something," she finished. "Bringing home a record for me or a present for Mom doesn't make up for it."

Mr. Thorne's eyes narrowed. "Oh, doesn't it?" His voice was quiet, controlled. That was always a danger signal.

Her stomach churned at the look on her father's face, but Hilary held up her chin. "No," she said, in a small but sturdy voice. "Money doesn't make up for unhappiness. And you make us all miserable."

Mr. Thorne erupted from behind the desk, knocking down his chair, and grabbed Hilary by the arm. He hustled her across the living room, moving so fast that Hilary stumbled, up the stairs and across the landing to her room. He threw open the door.

"So money's not important, is it?" he said through gritted teeth. "Shall we just dance through life with smiles on our faces? Would smiles have bought these drapes?" He grabbed one of them in his fist, ripped it off the curtain rod, and flung it to the center of the room. "Or these books?" With a sweep of his forearm, the books on Hilary's desk joined the drapes. "Or this?" He held up Hilary's new portable stereo.

"Daddy, no!" Hilary cried.

"Sam, stop!" Mrs. Thorne spoke sharply from the doorway. "What are you doing?"

"Hilary thinks money is no asset to life," said Mr.

Thorne. He tossed the stereo on the bed.

"I do not!" protested Hilary. "That's not what I said at all!"

"Well, I'd just like to see you try to get along without it," Mr. Thorne shouted right through her words.

"Well, you're the one who talked about destroying other people's property!" snapped Hilary.

"This is *my* property!" bellowed her father. "I earned the money for it, I paid for it, and it belongs to *me*!"

"Daddy, this is my room!" screamed Hilary. Tears—of anger, of fear, of anguish—flooded her cheeks.

"It is not *your* room! It is the room you are allowed to use in *my* house! And since you don't care for money, maybe I'll take some of the things my money paid for out of here!" Mr. Thorne's face was white, but his eyes were black with fury.

"Sam," interposed Mrs. Thorne finally, crossing the room and putting her hand on Mr. Thorne's shoulder. "Let's go downstairs and get something cool to drink."

Mr. Thorne shrugged off his wife's concern. "Oh, stop fussing, Carolyn," he said, but followed her out of the room. At the door, he turned and said to Hilary, "Clean up this mess."

Chapter Six

HILARY WAS CONSUMED BY FURY, RED AND HOT AND clashing with the cool blue bedroom.

"But I was trying to help!" she screamed down the stairs after them, then spun around and hammered the bed with her fists in frustration.

You're not supposed to punish people who're trying to do the right thing! He's wrong, I know he's wrong and I am right. He'll be sorry he didn't listen to me. They'll both be sorry someday—maybe when it's just too, too late. Yes, they'd be sorry then.

She turned purposefully to her bookcase. And I won't come back this time.

There was only a narrow strip of sand between the open river, dreaming peacefully under a blanket of stars, and the dark, mysterious bank, thick with undergrowth and menacing. Hilary made her way cautiously along it, picking her steps carefully, looking and listening.

I know where I ought to be, she thought, but it's best to be sure.

She waited. Presently a stealthy, short whistle disturbed the quiet. It came from the darkness of the bank. Nerves snapped to attention, Hilary whistled a low response.

"Who goes there?" A voice floated from the underbrush.

Hilary smiled. Safe. She knew exactly what to say. "Annie Bonney, scourge of the Caribbean!" she called out. "Name your name!"

"The Black Avenger of the Spanish Main!" cried the voice in terrible tones. A rustle in the trees disclosed a face, pale in the ghostly half-light of the night.

"Shiver me timbers!" cried this apparition in disgust. "You're no pirate, you're a girl!"

Hilary was quick to defend herself. "There *are* girl pirates, you know."

"Ho!" replied Tom Sawyer, emerging from shelter and presenting himself in all his freckled, tousled glory. "Durn'd if there are!"

Hilary stood her ground. "Durn'd to you, then, because there were. Some of 'em even more terrible and more famous than pirate men, so there! Annie Bonney was one, and so was Mary Read!" she said. "It's in the books!"

Tom was clearly glum at the prospect of admitting a girl, however bloodthirsty, into the sacred fraternal order of pirates, but if it was decreed by books, so it had to be, and he knew it.

"Well, all right, then," he said unwillingly. "Come this way." He turned and began to thread his way through thickets of scrub oak and yellow pine saplings, leaving Hilary to follow as best she could.

There were more ruffians at the camp, two of them, taking their ease around a bright fire and planning the next day's pillage. They looked up sharply when they heard Tom and Hilary approach, and put their hands at the ready on their belts.

"Who goes there?" barked one in a deadly voice.

"Tom," said Tom, unenthusiastically.

"Tom? We know no Tom! Give the countersign," demanded the other, jumping to his feet.

"Blood," said the Black Avenger, flatly. He walked into the clearing with Hilary.

His pirate band stared.

After a moment, recognition dawned over the second pirate's face. "A captive!" he cried jubilantly. "Tom, you never did!"

A gleam smote Tom. "Yes!" he cried. "A captive princess—"

"No!" protested Hilary, "I'm no princess! I'm a pirate, too!"

But Tom shook his head decidedly. "No," he said, "you have to be a hostage princess, captured from your native Zanzibar—" None of them had any idea where Zanzibar was, but the name had a handsome ring to it—"by the Spanish fleet, who were a-bearin' you back across the seas as a gift for their evil king when they met the broadsides from our cannon!"

He sprang to the alert and drew an imaginary cutlass, flourishing it about in a fierce and terrible manner. "The Spanish curs resisted—little knowing the power of the Avenger's wrath—they fired back—"

"Resist the Black Avenger, will ye?" cried the pirate king. "You'll rue the day, ha, ha! Raise the red flag, mates!"

Joe Harper, the Terror of the Seas, made as if to hoist the crimson banner up the mainmast of the pirate sloop, beneath the snapping Jolly Roger.

"Give no quarter!" The Avenger exhorted his crew. "Dead men tell no tales!"

Finn the Red-Handed brandished invisible long-barreled pistols in the face of the pretend enemy. "Aye," he hollered. "Show the bilge rats! Give 'em all ye got!"

Hilary drew her own weapon. "Swag-bellied

66

blighter!" she cried. "We will never surrender! Never!"

All the appropriate sound effects—the flash and boom of cannon and the ring of battle, the piteous cries of the vanquished and the brave shouts of the victors—echoed over the sleeping Mississippi from the fierce brigands in possession of Jackson's Island. Not until the light of day began to dim the flare of their pistol shots did the marauders declare the encounter won and collapse around the embers of their campfire.

"Build up the fire, wench," ordered Tom, waving an arm in the direction of their woodpile as he lolled against a convenient stump. "And fetch me grog!"

Hilary, in her role as captive princess, obeyed, then joined the others around the fire in easy democracy. "This is the life for me," she said dreamily. "I'm glad we all ran away."

"Nothin's better than this, I reckon," said Tom in satisfaction. "A pirate don't have to do nothin' he don't have a mind to do—"

"No one to pick on a fella," rejoined Huck feelingly.

"No nonsense here," said Joe. "Pirates believe a man when he gives his word. Why, it's a code of honor with them!"

"Right," said Tom. "We're best off here!"

"Right!" agreed the others.

"I don't ever want to go back," said Hilary sleepily.

"Here we are," continued Tom, somewhat drowsily, "and here we stay. We'll take an oath on it!"

"A blood oath," embellished Joe dreamily.

"Yes," said Tom. "The pirates of the Spanish Main will never darken *their* streets again. That'll learn 'em to toy with us!"

A snore was his only answer.

"Hilary, wake up! Hilary!"

An impatient hand rocked Hilary's shoulder. "Leave me alone, Avenger," she said irritably, and rolled after the sleep that ebbed away.

"Hilary. Wake. *Up!*"

Hilary gave in. "Okay! What is it?" she said at last, and opened her eyes.

The hand on Hilary's shoulder was not Tom Sawyer's, but her mother's.

"Hilary, are you all right?" Mrs. Thorne looked closely at her daughter. "It took me forever to wake you up. You almost scared me."

Sunlight flooded the room, drenched the bed, and rained upon the painted white furniture. A breeze through the open window made the curtains, cheerful on the worst of days, seem almost to laugh with joy, and the asparagus fern on the desk danced on the air. But the books still lay in a heap on the floor, and one of the curtains hung crazily.

Not Jackson's Island with Tom and Huck and Joe. Home, with Mom. And Dad. Hilary nearly cried with frustration. "Oh, what happened?"

"That's what I want to know," replied her mother. "It's almost noon, and you're still in bed. Do you have a fever?" She felt Hilary's forehead.

Hilary pulled away. "Leave me alone. I was just dreaming. You know you're never supposed to wake someone up in the middle of a dream."

"No, they get cranky, don't they?" agreed Mrs. Thorne. "Hilary, we need to talk."

"No, we don't." Hilary pulled the quilt protectively around her shoulders and turned toward the wall.

"Yes," insisted her mother, "we do." She turned the desk chair around to face the bed and sat down. She looked thoughtfully at Hilary's back.

"Hilary, I'm worried about you," she said.

That jerked Hilary around. She sat up to glare indignation at her mother. "Me!"

"Yes."

"*I'm* not the one causing a problem around here," Hilary said with some heat.

"I didn't say you were," replied her mother. "I said that I was worried about you. You're spending too much time shut up in this room."

She added, "I miss having you around."

Hilary picked at the threads of the quilt. There didn't seem to be an answer handy.

Her mother said gently, "Hilary, I know it hasn't been very pleasant around here lately, but believe me, problems aren't going to disappear just because you hide from them."

"I know that," Hilary broke in. "I know that, and I tried to fix it; I tried to tell Daddy what I thought was wrong, and it didn't work at all. He just got madder than ever." She dove under the covers.

Mrs. Thorne leaned over and shook her foot gently. "Hilary, come up here. What I'm trying to tell you is that Daddy's difficulties aren't the only ones we have to face around here. We also have yours." She pulled the covers back. Hilary rolled like a hedgehog to the bottom of the bed.

She replied without opening her eyes. "My difficulty is Daddy."

"No. Your problem is how you deal with Daddy—and with other people, too, by the way. You don't, you know."

Hilary opened her eyes. "I don't what?"

"You don't deal with other people. You run away from them."

"Well, maybe I don't need other people. Besides, if my own father can't stand me, how's anybody else going to?" Hilary's face tightened.

"Hilary, stop feeling sorry for yourself," Mrs. Thorne urged. "Get busy. Join a club at school, or go out for a team or something. Or get an afternoon job. Do anything, but do something. I'm going to take a Chinese class. Want to come? You'll make some friends, I'll bet."

"I've got all the friends I need." Hilary's fingers closed around the book by her pillow, and she began to burrow again.

But her mother took the book from her hand. "No, Hilary. I'm tired of this. Books are to you like whiskey is to a drunk. No books. Do things. Make friends."

"But you've always said that books enrich a person's life!" Hilary cried, panic rising in her throat.

"Enrich, yes, but you let them overwhelm you, Hilary. Read what you need to for school, but no more. For a while, anyway." Mrs. Thorne stood up.

Hilary said desperately, "Mom, wait! Let's talk about this!" She rolled off the bed and ran to the door ahead of her mother.

Mrs. Thorne looked very tired suddenly, stretched to the point of transparency. "Hilary, I've had enough conflict for one weekend. It's for your own good, believe me, please."

She moved Hilary gently to one side and went out, closing the door softly behind her.

Chapter Seven

AFTER LUNCH HILARY YELLED UP THE STAIRS TO the studio, "Mom, I'm going out to ride my bike!" She pulled open the back door, hoping to escape quietly. She hadn't forgiven her mother yet and didn't want to face her again.

"Hilary, wait!"

Hilary sighed.

Mrs. Thorne clattered down the wooden steps. "If you're going out, will you pick up some apples at the fruit farm?"

"Only what will fit in my backpack," Hilary answered curtly.

"That'll be plenty. Granny Smiths, if they have any. Need some money?"

"I've got some."

"Thanks!"

Hilary wheeled her bicycle down the gravel driveway to the road. The fruit farm lay beyond the town to the east, so she pointed her handlebars in that direction.

Freedom Hills was a very small town; just a village, really. A cluster of small buildings kept one another company around the stamp-sized square—a church, an antique shop, a pharmacy with a real old-fashioned soda fountain—but most businesses preferred the highway that arched north of town. There, shoppers thronged amid glass and concrete; here, the quiet buildings were either of fieldstone, great, gray rough rocks harnessed with painted wooden lintels and beams, or of clapboard, painted red, squat, low-ceilinged, with small windows and large chimneys. The grammar school even had a shell of logs, although the inside walls were plaster and the floors were modern vinyl. But whatever their recent embellishments, all the buildings were old, so old that the trees had grown up around them and woven their branches together above the chimneys, to care for the little structures and to shelter them. It was a nice, safe town—a quiet town.

Hilary rode straight down the main street on her way to the farm, but on the way home the cool air rushing at her face and the exercise made her thirsty and she decided to stop at the drugstore for a drink. She leaned her bicycle against one of the iron hitching posts, which still marched soldier-straight and solemn around the town square, and ran across the street and up the steps to the sidewalk.

The sidewalks of Freedom Hills had been created as an afterthought, a compromise between the thresholds of the various buildings, built high against the insults of dust and mud, and the road, worn low and rutted from centuries of use. As a result, one walked up stone steps from the road to the sidewalk, and up again to go inside a building. The sidewalks made the town unique and gave it character.

Hilary loved Freedom Hills. She loved the fat, placid houses, and the way the slate sidewalks rang in answer to her footsteps, and the fact that, if she squinted to blur the outlines of the cars parked on Main Street into the shapes of carts and carriages, she could see the town as it had looked two hundred years ago and earlier.

She walked down the street to the pharmacy. In Colonial times, thought Hilary dreamily, this town was almost new. That house on the corner with the black shutters probably had a man, maybe his sons, too, in the Battle of New York. Maybe they had a daughter my age. She'd take the eggs to the square on market day. What was her name? Prudence, I think. They liked those kinds of names back then.

Prudence enjoyed market day; there was a boy from one of the outlying farms she liked to meet, to talk to. She wore a blue dress and held its hem away from the mud with her free hand. It had rained last night. . . .

So absorbed was Hilary in the scene she was painting on the square that, when she opened the door of the pharmacy, the bright lights and noise caught her by surprise and almost sent her reeling into the street.

The twentieth century reclaimed Freedom Hills and vaporized the past with cool efficiency. Inside the store, video games clanked and whooped and a jukebox screamed in a corner. The lights were hot, bright despite the smoky air, and the place was packed with people.

Hilary stood in the doorway and stared at the gleaming soda fountain clear across on the opposite wall. If she went in, could she get out again? Her courage failed; she decided that she didn't want a drink, but some laughing kids came through the door behind her, and she was swept in with them.

Less conspicuous to go ahead, she thought, than to turn and run away. She began to make her way through the crowd.

"Excuse me," she said to a knot of nylon-jacketed boys standing by the games. "Excuse me!" she said, and one finally turned.

"Hey, Joe," he cried. "Don't you have ears? Excuse her! Let her through!" They jostled a little, and Hilary squeezed through. She could feel their eyes on her back as she passed. She shivered.

She hurried through the long aisle of booths and tables filled with talking girls. A boy bumped into her. "Hey, watch it!" he said.

"Sorry," she said.

The jukebox roared. Hilary found a stool at the counter, sat down, and ordered a lemonade to go. She took a deep breath and tried to relax her shoulders.

The kaleidoscope began to settle, giving Hilary a chance to see its separate elements. Some of these people she recognized from school: Amy, with her cascading flame of hair; Peter, her brother. They were tossing casual remarks to the boys at the games, laughing. That was Dennis, with the mustache. Amy's boyfriend, they said, but it was a secret because he was older and her parents didn't like him. So certain, so cool they are, thought Hilary. And so exciting. A secret boyfriend. I wonder if I could be like that. Like Mata Hari or someone. "Hey, Amy, what's new?" she thought experimentally. "How're you doing, Pete?"

Just then Peter glanced in Hilary's direction. Hilary smiled tentatively, but he looked away and murmured something to Amy, who laughed. Hilary felt warm, and turned away.

At a table a larger group of girls was giggling. "And her hair!" screeched one of them. The others joined in the squeals. Hilary's scalp tingled. She turned quickly toward the counter, without seeing the magazine the girls crowded around to point at. The noise floated behind her.

"She must cut it with a Lawn Boy!" Squeals, and fists drumming the table.

"And that nose," chimed another voice.

"She looks like she kissed the four-forty-five from Penn Station!" Screams.

Hilary's eyes swam. But what's wrong with my nose, she thought bewilderedly. I never thought—

"Here's your lemonade," broke in the counter-boy. "Eighty-five."

At last. "Oh. Oh, thanks," managed Hilary. She hauled up her backpack to dig for change.

She'd forgotten about the apples.

Three dozen Granny Smiths thumped, tumbled, and rolled across the floor, past the girls' table, over to Amy's booth, behind the jukebox, even out the door.

Apples were everywhere. In books there would have been a long, embarrassing silence, but there wasn't any silence here, just big noise and a bigger mess. Chagrined, Hilary jumped from the stool; she knocked over her lemonade, and a sea of sticky liquid washed over the apples rolling on the floor. People were stepping on the apples and cursing them, and sliding on the apples and yelling in alarm. Amy, on her way out the door, stumbled over one and gave Hilary a dirty look. One boy corralled half a dozen with a shout of triumph, but when Hilary held her hands out for them he began to juggle them, keeping them away from her. The others began to throw the rest of the apples around.

"Hey, look! Apple Frisbee!" An apple went careering through the air.

Someone else jumped up and caught it.

"Basket apple!" Another landed in the drawer of the cash register.

"Foot apple!" Tackle.

Girls screamed. Glass broke.

Hilary fled.

Chapter Eight

HILARY PEDALED FURIOUSLY TO CLEAR THE TOWN, but when she reached the country road her feet dropped off the pedals and the bicycle coasted. It wobbled finally to a stop on the side of a field. Hilary let go of the bike and threw herself face down in the dirt between rows of brown and broken stalks.

She covered her head with her hands and pressed her face into the dark and springy earth. She wasn't at all upset; every thought was clear and deliberate, and came in a precise, complete sentence.

Get me out of here, she thought. *GET ME OUT!* I need a hole to fall into. Oh, *please* give me a hole to fall into!

"Oh, dear, oh dear," said a thin, fretful voice at her elbow.

Hilary looked up. Sympathy?

A white rabbit in a striped satin waistcoat scurried away from her toward the opposite side of the field. "I'll be too late, too late," he said.

Rescue. With a sob of relief and without a backward glance, Hilary went after the animal and dove down the rabbit hole, hard on his heels.

It was dark and a long way down the rabbit hole, but otherwise very different from what Hilary had expected. It was a wide and airy cylinder with smooth, straight walls. Alice had plummeted down, she remembered, but Hilary wafted, gently, from side to side.

This isn't bad at all, she thought. Better, anyway, than up *there.* She hummed a little to pass the time and idly looked around.

Presently she noticed that the walls of the rabbit hole were not as completely smooth as she had thought, but were made up of tiny drawers stacked together like blocks. Each drawer had a handle notched into its front and bore a small white label neatly inscribed in black ink. Hilary tried to swing herself closer to the drawers so that she could read the labels, but found that the nearer she got to the walls the faster she fell, so she couldn't read the labels in any case.

One thing's for sure, she thought. It can't be a card catalogue. This isn't a library. Too dark.

She shivered suddenly. The rabbit hole had

branched, and now she was falling through a small passageway a good deal less airy and much darker than the big rabbit hole. She was deeper into the earth now, she figured; musty air rushed up her face and the wind was clingingly cold.

The ranks of drawers around the cylinder had given way to shelves, she noticed, packed to the cracking point with shadowy oddments covered with cobwebs and dusty with neglect. Hilary saw a bicycle, a pair of ice skates, stacks of books, a globe. She saw a golden apple and a meerschaum pipe.

Hey, I know this stuff, she thought. But what—?

A cement-hard floor knocked Hilary's breath away. A shower of apples thumped to earth around her and rolled off aimlessly.

She lay still a moment. Her teeth felt loose in her head, but the pain ebbed when she rubbed her face, and her breath came back to her. She sat up and looked around.

The rabbit hole had ended some fifteen feet or so above the floor, in the middle of a ceiling that looked like gray sponge, porous and thick and blotched with damp. The ceiling curved down to form the walls of a huge domed hall.

The air of the hall was crowded with smoke and movement and talk. Hilary heard laughter, a steady hum of voices, and music coming from across the room.

But she couldn't see anything.

She peered through the thick air to find a focal point, a face, maybe, or an object of any kind. The tendrils of smoke parted like curtains in front of her gaze, and she was able to see every inch of the floor and the high, curved walls.

She saw every inch of them because the room was perfectly empty. Empty—but she could hear people, just as though they were right in the room, and feel them moving around her.

A voice offered her a drink, which, mindful of Alice, she refused.

Then, in the corner of her eye she caught an image, a shadow of someone she recognized, someone she thought she knew. She whipped around to face it, but the image dissolved. It happened again; she spun around the other way—and again the shadow vanished.

She began to absorb wisps of the conversation that circled around her.

Her mother's voice said, "Hilary, why can't you make some friends?"

"You make me tired," came her father's words.

"I love to run," said Atalanta.

"Watson, look at this!"

"Merrily, merrily shall I live now!"

Hilary tried to shake away the voices. She was thoroughly frightened now; she looked wildly around for a means of escape.

A door appeared magically in the far wall of the room.

She ran for it, slammed the door behind her, and leaned against it to shut away the voices and the clamor in the hall.

She saw a flash of white at the end of the hallway. The rabbit, she thought. He must know the way out. She dashed after him, down two corridors and through a thick door, just as it swung shut.

Safe, she thought, and closed her eyes in relief.

But she'd hardly drawn breath when a voice rolled out in a wave from across the room. "Prisoner, approach the bench!"

Hilary looked up. She was in a courtroom. The light in the room was hot and harsh and came from a source behind a dark judge's bench that loomed toward the ceiling in front of her. To her left, a low railing of the same dark wood as the bench set apart an area lined across with small, hard chairs. To her right was a jury box, empty. The room was dusky and deserted, distorted by the opposition of the tall bench and the tiny chairs behind the rail. It smelled, too, like an old apartment house, like cooked onions and sadness.

Behind her, in the distance, Hilary could hear the shadowy voices, getting closer, coming after her. She tensed.

The voice in the room thundered again, this time accompanied by impatient rapping.

"Prisoner, approach the bench!"

Hilary craned her neck. The voice came from the very top of the judge's bench.

"Me?" she quavered.

"Speak up!" returned the voice peevishly. "Don't bleat! Yes, of course *you*. Do you see any other prisoner here?"

Hilary relaxed a little. The crankiness made the voice from the bench more ordinary and less frightening.

"The clerk will read the accusation," said the judge.

The courtroom door burst open and the voices surged in, but instead of swarming Hilary and engulfing her as she'd been afraid they would, they ranged themselves around the wooden railing and hung there in a murmur, waiting. The jury box stayed empty. Hilary felt a sense of relief at this. Perhaps the danger was less than she'd imagined.

"Order in the court! Clerk!"

One voice detached itself from the crowd and floated toward the judge's bench. Hilary didn't recognize this one.

"Hilary Louise Thorne," the voice rang out in solemn tones, "you stand accused of failure. Why can't you be like everybody else?"

I wish I knew, thought Hilary.

The voice dropped its official tone and said conversationally, "No wonder everyone makes fun of you. I just can't believe what you did with those apples."

"Neither can I." Hilary sighed. I guess I deserve whatever I get, she thought. But whatever it is has to be better than facing those kids in school on Monday.

The clerk reverted to a formal voice. "Have you anything to say for yourself?"

A violent hammering came from the bench. "That's my line!" the judge protested.

"Well, say it, then," replied the clerk. "What's keeping you?"

"Have you anything to say for yourself?" barked the judge.

Hilary was dazed by the speed with which the judge changed personalities. "What do you want me to say?" she asked faintly.

"Are you guilty or not?"

"I suppose I am," Hilary said. "But—"

The spectator voices drowned her out, and the judge rapped them silent.

"Very considerate of you, I'm sure," he said to Hilary. "Saves us the expense of a jury, not to mention the persecutor."

"Prosecutor, you idiot!" cried the clerk.

The judge huffed. "Same thing!"

"No, it's not! We do still need the persecutor. She has to be punished, you know."

Hilary laughed incredulously.

The judge turned to her hopefully. "Would you care to do that, too? These budget cuts, you know."

Hilary lost her patience. "What kind of place is this, anyway?" she demanded. "Who are you, and where am I?"

The clerk's voice became crafty. "Can't you guess?"

"No, I can't guess!" shouted Hilary. "Who are all these voices?"

"You should know. You brought them here," answered the clerk.

"I did not," said Hilary flatly. She was angry now.

"Yes, you did. They're yours. Your memories, your people, your things. Everyone you ever met and remembered. Everything you know."

"Who are you, anyway?"

"Don't you know?"

Hilary felt cold.

"No, I suppose not," continued the clerk. "No one can ever recognize his own voice."

"You're me?"

"Who else would be so hard on you?"

Hilary began to cry. "I don't understand! Please tell me where I am! Am I out of my mind?"

"You're in your mind, Hilary."

The voices began to close around her.

Hilary couldn't breathe. "Get away," she

screamed, pushing at them as they hedged her in. "Get away! Get away!"

She began to flail her fists to beat them off and found herself beating off the icy raindrops that had begun to pelt the countryside around Freedom Hills.

She sat there on the grass for a moment in the rain, then rose, righted her bicycle, and started for home.

Chapter Nine

THE WHEELS OF THE BIKE SCREAMED ON THE WET pavement, jeering at her. Crazy Hilary, crazy, they sang over and over again. Crazy. Crazy. Crazy.

What other explanation could there be? I *must* be nuts, she thought distractedly. There weren't any books this time, just— She groped for the right word. The delusion. Yes. Fantasy. Yes. It's all just fantasy from a demented mind.

Rain dribbled down the back of her neck, and tails of hair plastered themselves to her face, but Hilary barely noticed.

Maybe there never was any magic, she thought, wiping the back of her hand across her eyes. Maybe I've always been nuts, and just lucky that no one has noticed. Pretty soon, though, somebody's going to figure it out, and then I'll be in for it. They'll shut me away from the world, probably in a crumbling tower where I can't hurt anyone, and I'll spend my days and nights drifting along the twisting stairwell in rotting draperies and singing to myself in a high, cracked voice—

Stop! Oh, just stop it, she cried to herself, and laughed almost hysterically. Haven't you had enough for one day?

She bent her head and pedaled harder through the downpour.

The road banked in a curve around a small cottage nestled in a blaze of oak and sugar maple, which looked warm and safe from the storm. As Hilary coasted around it she heard a voice call out her name.

"Hilary? Hilary Thorne?"

No more voices for me, Hilary thought. She was determined not to answer.

A mushroom figure, short legs under a huge umbrella, dashed from the cottage to the road and stood in her path, waving. Hilary could cither hit the figure or stop, so, reluctantly, she stopped.

It was Mrs. Kane, the English teacher.

"Child," she said. "It ain't a fit night out for man or beast, as they say. Come in out of the rain."

"Oh, it's okay, Mrs. Kane," Hilary replied. She was surprised at the perfectly normal sound of her own voice. "I won't melt."

But Mrs. Kane insisted. "Think of the driver

who'd hit you. Do you want to spend eternity on his conscience? Come in, child; come in!"

Just like in school, where she always just assumed that you'd do exactly what she told you to and never gave you a chance to do anything else, Mrs. Kane turned back to the house. Hilary followed helplessly. Her sneakers squished and oozed along the path to the front door.

"I'm afraid I'm going to make a mess in your house," she said, but Mrs. Kane shook her head.

"It doesn't matter," she said, and opened the door.

Hilary looked around in surprise. "It's beautiful!" she said. "Oh, what a wonderful home!"

The entire first floor of the cottage was taken up by the friendliest kitchen Hilary had ever seen. Cabinets, countertops, and floor were golden wood, rubbed to a glow; cheerful rag rugs, curtains, and the polished copper pots and bunches of dried flowers that hung from the rafters added color to the warmth. A fire burned merrily in a huge brick fireplace that had an easy chair beside it and a roomy table, stacked with books, in front of it.

"I like it," replied Mrs. Kane. "Let's have something to eat. Do you like sausage?"

It sounded good. "Yes, please," said Hilary. "Can I help?"

"Yes," said Mrs. Kane, tipping the steaming contents of a saucepan into two heavy earthenware mugs. "You can sit by the fire and drink this cocoa."

Hilary settled at the table in front of the hearth. She watched Mrs. Kane move between stove and countertop and listened to the crackle of the fire. "It's nice here," she said shyly. "You only need a dog to make it picture perfect."

"Oh, heavens." Mrs. Kane put down the skillet with a clatter, opened the door, and began to croon in a wheedling tone quite unlike her normal tart voice, "Come on, Max. Come on, boy, you can do it, come on!"

Hilary got up. "Who is it?" she asked. "Who's Max?"

"My picture-perfect dog," Mrs. Kane said wryly.

At the bottom of the steps stood the largest and wettest dog Hilary had ever seen—definitely larger than a Great Dane, just a shade smaller than a pony. It had short, fawn-colored hair feathered with black at the tips of its ears, tail, and muzzle, and a noble, square head that at the moment hung incongruously between his knees.

"What is it?" asked Hilary, awed.

"An English mastiff," Mrs. Kane replied. "Believe it or not, they've been considered the bravest dogs in existence for more than a thousand years. Come on, Max!"

The dog didn't budge. "Why won't he come up?" asked Hilary.

"He's afraid of the stairs," said Mrs. Kane with

exasperation. "Has been ever since he slipped on them during the ice storm last year. I think the fall addled his wits. He's also afraid of falling leaves, all people, some squirrels, the telephone bell, and mirrors. Come *on*, Max!"

But the poor animal stood still, shivering, his great, soft eyes fixed on the lowermost step.

Hilary wasn't afraid of animals, thanks to her experiences with Ratty and Mole and the others, so she said, "I'll get behind and nudge him, if you want."

Mrs. Kane chuckled. "It'll be like nudging Mount Rushmore," she warned. "I'll pull while you push."

With effort and giggling they got Max over the threshold, and as soon as they did he made a beeline for the kitchen table and, crouching in abject terror of the stranger in his house, burrowed between the chairs until he reached shelter beneath the tabletop.

Hilary laughed delightedly. "Now he thinks that we can't see him!" The homey smell of damp dog rose gently in the room.

Mrs. Kane surveyed the tip of Max's tail with foreboding. "Wait until he stands up. Then we'll see more than enough. Everything on the table will go flying. Well, let's eat. Sit down, child."

Hilary toed off her shoes and curled her damp feet in Max's coat. She felt completely at home after the tussle with the dog. "This is the nicest I've felt in a long time," she said happily.

Mrs. Kane set a plate of sliced sausages, cheese and crackers, and fruit in front of Hilary.

"More cocoa?" asked Mrs. Kane.

"Yes, please," said Hilary.

Mrs. Kane sat down opposite Hilary with her own plate, and they ate in companionable silence.

"This is wonderful cheese, Mrs. Kane," Hilary said at length. "Are these chives?"

"No. Thyme, from my garden last summer," replied Mrs. Kane. "My vacation project was to learn to dry herbs properly. Did you know that the ancients believed that herbs and spices had magical properties? Poppy seeds were supposed to make you invisible, they said, and if a lady sprinkled cumin on a man's food he would love her for the rest of his life. They even had a cure for baldness—rosemary. Works every bit as well as the ones we have today."

Hilary laughed. "What does thyme do?" she asked.

"Among other things, it cures nightmares."

Hilary chewed with interest.

Mrs. Kane got up to pour more cocoa, then sat down again and leaned back comfortably in her chair. "So, child," she began, "would you like to talk about it?"

Hilary didn't even bother to ask how the teacher knew that something was wrong. She knew Mrs. Kane. The fire popped, and Max sighed and shifted under her feet. Hilary played with her mug, twisting it so that the handle was aligned perfectly with the grain of the tabletop. "I think I'm crazy," she said at last.

Mrs. Kane didn't laugh. "Why?" she said simply.

"I have these dreams," answered Hilary. "Well, not dreams, really, because I'm not asleep. I used to think they were magic travels, but the last one just sort of came on its own, and now I don't know what to do—"

"Wait," commanded the teacher. "Tell me the whole story. Begin at the beginning, and go on until you come to the end; then stop."

The quotation from *Alice in Wonderland* made Hilary wince, but she took the advice. "It started a long time ago, when I first learned to read."

Mrs. Kane listened quietly, one hand rhythmically kneading Max's neck. When Hilary was finished, she got up silently, refilled the mugs, and threw another log on the fire. "Well," she said at last, "what makes you think you're insane?"

Hilary almost choked on her cocoa. "Weren't you listening?"

"Certainly I was," replied Mrs. Kane imperturbably. "And it seems to me that, as Shakespeare said in *Hamlet:* 'Though this be madness, yet there is method in't.' Child, what do you think insanity is?"

"Well, I don't know the textbook definition, but I should think that experiencing magic trips into other worlds would qualify," said Hilary, a little nettled at the teacher's serenity.

"By that definition, then, practically any writer or painter or poet would be mad. They all create their own worlds, you know."

"No," said Hilary positively, "because that's creativity. It's their imaginations."

"Yes," said Mrs. Kane.

After a moment, Hilary saw the teacher's point. "No," she said, shaking her head, "my trips are definitely not my imagination."

"Why not?"

Hilary said, "If it's all my imagination, how come the library smelled like Sherlock Holmes's tobacco, and how come there was an oak leaf in my hair from getting Toad down?" She felt triumphant. "That's evidence."

"Of what? You did walk through the woods that day?"

"Well, yes," Hilary admitted.

"And your dad does smoke a pipe?"

"Yes," she said, in a very small voice.

"Those sound like perfectly good explanations to me," said Mrs. Kane calmly.

Hilary was silent for a moment. "So I am crazy."

"I didn't say that. What's the difference between

a 'magic' trip and an 'imagined' one?" Mrs. Kane challenged her.

Hilary wrinkled her forehead. "Magic can send you places you've never been, it can create something out of nothing, it can make you accomplish what seems impossible," she began.

"And imagination?" prompted Mrs. Kane.

"Well, your imagination can take you places you've never been—" Hilary stopped. "Hey, I never thought of that. Your imagination *takes* you, but magic *sends* you."

Mrs. Kane nodded in approval. "Exactly. There's quite a difference between going somewhere and being sent there."

"Control, I guess," said Hilary. "You're in control of your imagination, and magic is in control of you."

"Yes," said Mrs. Kane. "And imagination is the more powerful, because you can direct it. If you're under a magic spell, you're just a pawn."

Neither of them spoke for a moment. Mrs. Kane got up and went over to the window. "It looks like the clouds are breaking up," she commented.

Hilary said, "But, Mrs. Kane, what about that last trip? I don't think I was in control of that one."

Mrs. Kane shrugged. "I think you were. It sounded as though you were punishing yourself."

"But there weren't any books around and I traveled anyway!"

"Once you've read a book it's always with you. Sometimes I'm reminded years later of stories I've read. And it seems that your travels have become almost automatic for you."

"I suppose so," said Hilary.

"There's nothing too wrong with that," said Mrs. Kane. "We all have to have ways of coping with unpleasantness. No one can stand in the sun without a hat for very long. I'll bet that putting on a hat—escaping, in other words—has become almost automatic for you." She added, more gently, "It's hard on everyone to move to a strange place, but most especially an only child."

Hilary was confused at the change of subject. "I'm not sure what you mean," she said.

The teacher laughed. "You're unique, but not unhinged," she said. "You have the gift of imagination, child. All you have to do is learn how to master it. It's more powerful than you think."

They went outside. The sunlight made a prism of each remaining raindrop, and the world, gray before, was filled with color.

"Well, thanks, Mrs. Kane, I guess," said Hilary, getting on her bicycle. "I kind of did like being magic, though. It was better than just being different."

"I think you'll like being talented just as much." Mrs. Kane smiled. "Give it a chance."

Chapter Ten

MONDAY MORNING.

Lockers clanged.

"Hey, Apples!"

Hilary cringed. A shape loomed beside her. "I have your backpack," it said.

Hilary looked up, surprised at the pleasant tone. Amy's brother, Peter, smiled and held out the bag.

"Thanks," said Hilary softly.

"You gave us an afternoon to remember, that's for sure," he said. "It was great. I can't remember when I've laughed so hard. Where did all those apples come from, anyway?"

"Eppler's Fruit Farm," replied Hilary dazedly, surprised at the attention. "It's a self-serve place. You can even press the apples yourself if you want cider."

"Do you go there a lot?"

"We squeeze it in every once in a while," said Hilary, almost involuntarily.

Peter laughed. "I guess I asked for that one. I never would have thought of you as punny, you look so intense and serious all the time. Listen, can I go there with you sometime? You make it sound so ap-peeling!"

Hilary grinned suddenly. "Of cores!"

Peter laughed again. "Great." The bell rang. "Oh, geez. I'm late again. See you!"

Peter flew down the stairs, and Hilary stared after him.

Chapter Eleven

HILARY WAS IN A THOUGHTFUL MOOD WHEN SHE helped her mother clean up the breakfast dishes the following Saturday morning. "I can't figure out this friend-making business, Mom," she said. "It seems like if I don't worry about it, I get along just fine, but when I begin to wonder about what other people think of me, everything gets all weird."

Mrs. Thorne said, "I think that happens to everybody."

"Carolyn!" Mr. Thorne appeared in the doorway in a suit and tie, dressed for work. "Where are my car keys?"

"Wherever you left them," Mrs. Thorne replied evenly.

"Daddy, why are you all dressed up on Saturday?"

"I left them on my dresser. You moved them!"

"Sam, I haven't seen your car keys."

"Daddy, are you going to work *today*? Aren't you ever going to stay home again?"

"Do you think the keys would just drive off of their own accord?"

"I think you misplaced them," said Mrs. Thorne carefully.

"Daddy—"

"Hilary, be quiet!"

Hilary threw the dishcloth on the floor and stalked out of the kitchen and into the library. Her father's briefcase, car keys tossed on top, was on the desk as usual, and she carried it into the kitchen like a tray, setting it down with ceremony on the table in front of her father. She returned to the library in dignified silence and closed the door behind her.

Then she dropped dejectedly into her father's chair. Mr. Thorne hadn't gotten around to buying a new one yet; it was the same shabby Mount Everrest, smelling faintly of Walnut tobacco, of pencil shavings, of coffee. Hilary suddenly, sharply, ached with longing for her father. I want him back, she thought as the ache sharpened to piercing point, the father I used to have, the one who taught me to read, to pun, to play—he loved me. I need that.

101

Stop feeling sorry for yourself, she admonished herself resolutely. That won't bring him back.

Bring him back—she sat up. That's it! She rolled out of the chair to her feet and to the bookcases with a single motion. She reached for a large and tattered book of fairy tales, so worn it was held together with masking tape and library paste. She carried it gently to the couch.

It's been a while, she thought, but if this story is the way I remember it—she opened it gingerly.

Slowly the book-lined walls of the library melted into a mist of green and Hilary found herself on a country lane. Meadows stretched beyond the fences on either side of her, and the lane reached out to hills. Hilary saw in front of her a boy about her own age who trudged slowly down the lane with a bundle on his back. She ran after him.

"Jack, wait!" she called.

But the boy didn't stop. "I'm off to the sea to seek my fortune!" he called back over his shoulder. "Don't try to stop me!"

Hilary caught up with him and fell into step beside him. "But why?"

"I made a pretty mess of things here. My poor mother's at her wits' end," he said glumly, "and I don't blame her. First my father's taken prisoner by the giant, and then I must needs play the knave."

"Oh." Hilary nodded. "The cow."

Jack flushed. "Does everyone in the village already know? Oh, I grant you it was silly of me, but I had to take the chance. If the magic beans had worked—"

"I know what you mean," said Hilary.

"But now, no cow, no nothing. Nothing but a handful of worthless beans." Jack shifted his bundle to the other shoulder. "I must make it up to my mother somehow."

"But, Jack," said Hilary. "You believed in those beans when you got them, right?"

"Aye." Jack nodded unhappily.

"Well, the beans haven't changed any. Have you?"

"I've made myself a laughingstock."

"Don't worry about other people," urged Hilary. "Follow your own path. Give the beans a chance."

Jack looked puzzled. "What do you mean?"

"Plant them," said Hilary promptly. "See what happens."

Jack reached into his pocket and drew out the seven magic beans. They lay withered and drab and uninspiring on his palm. "I suppose I could," he said doubtfully.

"Do," pressed Hilary. "I'll help."

Jack put his bundle down by the side of the road, and he and Hilary put the beans in a shallow hole there and covered them with a small pile of dirt.

Some water was in the bottom of a ditch that ran alongside the road, and this they carried up to the seedbed in cupped hands.

"Now what?" said Jack, when they had finished.

"Now we wait," said Hilary. "There's a grassy spot over there. Let's sit down."

But as they turned away they heard a rumbling, roaring sound deep within the earth, and they looked back at their digging. The ground trembled and bubbled there as though it boiled. The rumbling grew louder, mounting in pitch to an unbearable height.

Suddenly the noise cracked, the ground broke open, and one seedling, its leaves first pale, then growing vivid green, shot into daylight. While Jack and Hilary watched in amazement, the seedling grew as fast as running water into a tall stalk, straight up toward the sky, and then it sprouted broad, strong leaves as evenly spaced as the rungs of a ladder.

The invitation was unmistakable.

Jack and Hilary climbed the beanstalk rapidly, lifting themselves above the town and above the trees and above the hills into the sky. Soon damp and misty clouds closed in around them, shutting out the sun. Their hands grew cold and their fingers numb, but the beanstalk stretched higher yet, so Jack and Hilary climbed on.

They broke through the clouds suddenly, without warning, and were dazzled by the sunlight. Hilary put a hand up to shade her eyes. "What's there?" she said to Jack. "Can you see?"

Jack squinted, then took his breath in sharply. " 'Tis the castle of the giant! That's where my father is!"

Jack's voice was a little uneven on the last words, but his confidence had begun to flow back in waves since the beans had proven magic after all. "And I'm going to get him out!"

Hilary said succinctly, "I'll help." Jack nodded.

They made their way among the tussocks of clouds carefully. Presently the castle wall loomed before them, and they walked along its line until they reached a door made of oak trees lashed together with iron straps and rivets. It stood so high they could not reach the latch.

Jack pushed against the door. It didn't budge. "How do we get in?"

A bellpull hung beside the door. Hilary grinned mischievously. "We'll just have to ring the bell!"

Jack crouched down and Hilary climbed on his shoulders. She stretched until her fingers reached the bell rope. A clang sounded deep inside the castle, and heavy footsteps answered it.

Hilary and Jack scrambled behind a bulge in the wall.

A dark and evil-looking giant pulled the big door open. "Aye," he said. "Who is't?"

He came out a few paces to look around, and Jack and Hilary slipped inside behind him. They ran for a dark corner of the vast entrance hall and waited.

When the giant had satisfied himself that there was no one there, he stomped back inside and slammed the door, muttering under his breath. He moved off down one of the stone corridors. Hilary and Jack shadowed him.

They followed him into the castle dining room, where the table was set for a meal for one. The giant lifted a gilded cage from the sideboard and laughed heartily. "Fe, fi, fo, fum," he boomed.

> *"I smell the blood of an Englishman;*
> *Be he alive or be he dead,*
> *I'll grind his bones to make my bread."*

Inside the cage was a man who beat exhaustedly against the bars.

Jack grabbed Hilary's arm. "That's my father!"

"But first," the giant said, "a little entertainment to stimulate the appetite."

"We need a plan," whispered Hilary.

"We don't have time for a plan," replied Jack desperately. "If you see a chance, grab it."

The giant had produced from a cupboard a flute of polished wood and a metal tray upon which a gray goose sat.

"Lay, goose, lay!" cried the giant, and the goose clucked forth a golden egg, which the giant tossed like a shuttlecock from hand to hand.

"Play, flute, play!" cried the giant, and the flute wavered in the air and piped a stately waltz. The giant swayed ponderously and hummed along with the flute; then he began to twirl slowly.

He was dancing in time to the music.

"Faster, flute, faster!" Jack cried out suddenly, and the flute obeyed, whistling merrily and whirling the giant around the room faster and faster and out of control until he fell down flat in a dizzy faint.

"Quick," said Jack. He ran to the cage and rattled its door impatiently. "It's locked!"

His father raised a hand, but he was too weak to help.

"Here!" said Hilary. She handed him one of the giant's enormous spoons, and Jack smashed it against the lock of the cage until the lock broke.

The cage door swung open, and Hilary and Jack half carried, half dragged Jack's father through it.

Hilary shot a glance at the giant, who groaned. "He's coming to!" she said. "Let's go!"

Jack and Hilary pelted down the corridors of the castle with Jack's father between them, the goose that laid the golden eggs and the magic flute close on their heels and the giant thundering behind them. The procession got shorter as the giant gained ground.

"This way!" Jack panted as they reached the giant door, and the parade snaked toward the beanstalk. They dove for it and slid down, first Jack with his father, then Hilary with the flute in her pocket. The goose came last, pinfeathers flying, just as the giant leaped and made a grab for the tip of the beanstalk.

But he was too heavy. The beanstalk cracked.

It snapped at the base and swayed slowly, first one way and then the other as the giant clung in peril at the top. While Hilary and Jack and his father watched in awe, the beanstalk shuddered, toppled, and finally banished the giant to the middle of the sea a league away.

Chapter Twelve

HILARY FOUND HER MOTHER ON THE PORCH WITH some pumpkins arrayed in a semicircle on the table in front of her. The air was brisk, and the pumpkins brought inside some of the lively color on the trees and autumn flowers outside. Mrs. Thorne wore a bright, thick sweater and an industrious expression.

"Oh, Hilary, come in," she welcomed when she saw her daughter in the doorway. "I want to do something creative with these things for the Oktoberfest at school. Any suggestions?"

Hilary studied the pumpkins. "How about the Seven Dwarfs?"

"Oh, good idea," her mother approved. "I even know them all, too. Bashful-Grumpy-Sneezy-Happy-Dopey-Sleepy-Doc."

Hilary laughed. "You've been playing too many trivia games, Mom."

"Trivia games, nothing," protested Mrs. Thorne. "I've seen that movie twenty-three times in my long and useful life."

Hilary dropped a kiss on her mother's hair as she circled the table to reach a vacant chair. "A useful life, indeed," she agreed.

Her mother was pleasantly surprised. "You're pretty chipper this afternoon. What's the occasion?"

"No occasion. I just think we haven't been very nice to each other lately."

"You have a point there." Although she spoke lightly, a cloud passed over Mrs. Thorne's expression.

"Is Daddy home yet?"

"He said he'd be home before supper." Mrs. Thorne picked up a black crayon.

"Mom, I have a great idea," said Hilary eagerly. "Let's have a picnic tonight, up on Lenape Mountain."

"Oh, Hilary, it's awfully chilly for a picnic," said her mother, outlining a crooked grin on the blank face of one pumpkin.

"But it's still light until late. And we can build a bonfire. It'll be fun. We can roast potatoes and take along some cider or something and watch the stars come out."

"Oh, I don't know," her mother demurred.

"Come on, Mom," Hilary said softly, persuasively. "Daddy could use some time outdoors, I bet."

"True," admitted Mrs. Thorne. She gave the pumpkin a button-bright eye and looked at the face consideringly. "Well, why not? It'd probably do us all some good," she said at last.

"Terrific," said Hilary, bouncing up. "I'll get everything ready."

She went inside, and Mrs. Thorne called after her, "I think the campfire grill is buried in the basement somewhere."

Hilary went downstairs and found the grill hanging from a rafter with her father's fishing tackle. She unhooked it, then, on a whim, also unhooked the fishing gear and brought that upstairs, too, singing to herself as she came.

When Mr. Thorne came through the front door early that evening, Hilary was ready for him.

"Hi, Daddy," she said, standing on tiptoe to kiss his cheek. "Hurry up and get ready. Mom has your clothes laid out."

"Get ready for what?" asked Mr. Thorne, bewildered. "Where are we going?"

"Out," said Hilary. "Don't ask any questions. It will all become clear in due time." She pushed him toward the stairs and chuckled mysteriously.

He came downstairs wearing the old flannel

shirt Hilary liked so much, and the three of them piled in the car. Mrs. Thorne drove.

"I wish you'd tell me what you two are up to," said Mr. Thorne testily. "I've got a lot of work to do tonight. I don't have time for games."

Neither Hilary nor her mother answered, and Mr. Thorne's irritation turned into surprise as Mrs. Thorne pulled into a clearing at the base of the mountain. "Lenape Mountain! I haven't thought of this place in ages!"

"It used to take us hours to get here from the old house, and we came all the time," Mrs. Thorne observed. "Now it only takes us minutes, and we haven't been here in months."

"And that's months too long," said Hilary, handing her father a backpack. "Remember the first time you brought me here?"

"Do I ever!" He laughed. "You'd never been fishing before, but you hooked just about every trout in the stream and left your poor old man to sing for his supper! Talk about beginner's luck!"

"It wasn't luck. I had a good teacher," Hilary said. "I brought your fishing tackle today, too." She took a fishing-rod bag from the back of the car.

Her father shook his head in protest. "Oh, no, no! Don't drag out all that junk. I don't have the time tonight. Besides," he said with an air of surprise, as if remembering a long-forgotten fact, "the fish are spawning. They won't be interested in food."

Hilary went on. "I brought your waders, too, and everything else I could remember." She busied herself in the bottom of the trunk. "Uh-oh. I did forget something."

"Oh, well, don't worry about it. I don't want to fish, anyway," said Mr. Thorne quickly. "Come on, come on, let's get this show on the road here."

Hilary brought her head out of the trunk and opened her mouth, but an idea struck her and she shut it abruptly.

"Okay, Daddy," she said meekly.

Mrs. Thorne looked suspiciously at Hilary, but said nothing.

They all picked up backpacks and bundles and set out single file along the trail. Dry leaves crackled under their feet, and the air was sharp in their nostrils.

"There's no place cleaner than a mountainside in autumn," Mrs. Thorne said happily as they tramped along. "And that seems silly, really, when you think about it, because there really isn't anything fresh or new about fall—everything is old and dying."

Mr. Thorne said thoughtfully, "No, I think you're right. It *is* a clean time—or at least a simple time, especially when you compare it with the summer, when there's so much growing on."

Hilary grinned. It was just like old times.

They walked on. Mr. Thorne added after a

while, "Autumn cleans up after the summer. The dying plants make the food for the next year's growth."

Mrs. Thorne said idly, "Speaking of food, I wonder if there's a class around in wild-food gathering. Supposedly it's possible to live entirely on wild plants even in this day and age. Dandelion greens, horehound root—that sort of thing."

Hilary said quickly, "I think I'll take over the cooking for a while."

Mr. Thorne laughed but said, "Maybe it wouldn't be so bad to eat more naturally."

Hilary said, "It isn't the root to my heart."

The sound of the river reached them then, and they followed it, taking a split in the trail that led to a clearing near the bank. They found a square, flat rock there to use as a campfire bed, so they lowered their packs to the ground and stretched their shoulders.

"Look," said Hilary softly. "On the log across the river."

A raccoon was perched on a branch of a fallen log that skimmed the waterline. It peered at the water below it with bright, inquisitive eyes, watching the few insects that played there. Suddenly its hands shot out and scooped a fish from a metallic flash of water. The animal chirruped at its prize, gave it a triumphant swish in the water, and carried it off toward the opposite bank.

"Just like *Rascal,*" Hilary breathed. "Like a person!"

"Raccoons are intelligent animals," said her father. "Did you see the way it watched the bugs on the water, as if it knew they'd attract the fish?"

"Just like you, Dad, except that it uses real flies and you use artificial ones!"

"Oh, it's better than I am!" said Mr. Thorne. "It has to hunt the flies before it hunts the fish, and it *still* makes a living at it!"

"Speaking of flies," said Mrs. Thorne, who had been digging through their backpacks, "did our supper grow wings? It seems to be missing."

"Oh, gee, I must have forgotten to put the cooler bag in the car," said Hilary expressionlessly.

Mrs. Thorne raised her eyebrows.

"Well," said Mr. Thorne mildly, his eyes on the river, "maybe I can catch our dinner."

"Oh, yes, Daddy!" cried Hilary enthusiastically. "Here's your rod."

"I wondered why you lugged that fly rod all the way up from the car," murmured Mrs. Thorne to her daughter while Mr. Thorne got his fishing gear from Hilary's pack and fitted the pieces of his fishing rod together. "Did you 'forget' on purpose?"

Hilary whispered, "No, but when I realized that I had, I thought I'd take a chance on the fishing stuff."

Mrs. Thorne tousled her daughter's hair.

Hilary ran after her father to the river's edge. "What kind of lure are you going to use, Daddy?"

"A mayfly, I think. It's the only thing I have that's likely to fool the fish at this time of year." He stretched out an arm to point at a streak of dark water that ended at a rotting stump and a riffle of rocks some distance down the stream. "See there? That's deep pocket water, and I bet you there's a nice big rock underwater there that's an old trout family homestead. And you see those bushes that hang over the dark area, there? That's just the kind of place mayflies like to hide. So, if we cast our fly just right, right there, not even the smartest fish will have any idea that it's a fake."

Hilary opened the fly box and lifted out a lure. "Here's a mayfly."

"Yes, but it's too big," said her father. "At this time of year, mayflies are much smaller." He reached into the box. "This one will do."

"I still can't believe you have to know all this stuff just to catch a dumb fish," said Hilary.

"Trout have survival instincts like any other creature," replied her father, tying his fly to the leader on the fly line. "A fisherman has to be awfully good to get a fish to let down its guard, and, as in any contest, to be good you've got to know as much as you can about your opponent."

Mr. Thorne waded into the water. "If you do

catch a fish, it's because, for a minute, you're part of its world. It's like being accepted into a very secret society. You feel as if you belong."

He made a few experimental casts with his rod, not allowing the fly to touch the water. "It's been a long time since I've done this," he said with pleasure.

With a smooth motion, he lifted the fly rod and its line up and just over his head. The line sailed out behind him. He brought his arm slowly in front of his body, and the fly line looped and began to surge forward, unrolling and straightening itself. As the line dropped, Mr. Thorne pulled his arm back again, and the fly just kissed the water before the line picked it up and carried it back to its starting point to repeat the pattern that had just been formed.

The motion was as intricate as ballet, and as graceful. Hilary watched her father, hip deep in water and motionless except for his arms, and thought about how much a part of the stream he looked. He does belong here, she thought, with the fish and the animals and all the nature things he knows about and loves.

Mrs. Thorne had come to stand beside Hilary and seemed to have the same thoughts, for she said, "He withers in the city, doesn't he?"

"Here we go," Mr. Thorne said calmly. The rod bowed, and he pulled it up sharply to set the hook.

The fish surfaced in a spray of molten silver, thrashing and fighting the line, then took off downstream, weaving back and forth across the current and doubling back in a frenzied effort to free itself. It headed for a thorny stump on the bank and tried to break the line, but Mr. Thorne reeled it in a little with a chuckle, saying, "Not my line you won't, sir." Other than that, the man let the fish run.

When the fish finally tired, Mr. Thorne brought it in slowly. Hilary and her mother knelt on the bank to watch. "Oh, it's *huge!*" said Hilary. "I've never seen one so big!"

It was big. A solid rainbow over two feet long, and nearly eight pounds, they thought. Mr. Thorne put his net in the water and guided the fish over it. He held it there and looked at his wife hopefully.

"It's really too big for us to eat in one meal, Carolyn," he said.

Mrs. Thorne smiled. "Much too big," she agreed. "Why don't you let it go and see if you can get a smaller one?"

Mr. Thorne reached into the net and twisted the hook out of the mouth of the fish. The fish floated still for a few moments, but revived presently and swam away as Hilary and her mother and her father watched.

"Take it easy, slugger," said Mr. Thorne softly after it. He prepared to cast again. "It might be a while, Carolyn," he warned.

"Okay by me," his wife replied. "Hilary, let's gather some wood for the fire."

They lounged around their campfire rock for a long while after they'd eaten. "There's nothing as good as this," Hilary purred, her head on her mother's lap. "Let's stay here always. Dad can fish and you can collect your weeds and I'll—I'll coordinate things."

Mr. Thorne poked idly at the fire with a stick. "I wish we could stay here," he said. "I feel as though I've come back to where I belong."

The fire cracked and settled.

"Do you think you belong here, Mom?" Hilary asked absently, mesmerized by the coals.

Mrs. Thorne thought for a while. "Yes," she said at last, "but then, I always do. Wherever I am."

Silence threaded through their clearing. "Angels passing," said Hilary.

Mr. Thorne tossed his stick on the fire. "I don't," he said. "I feel like I fit into things about as well as a size-eight foot in a size-twelve shoe."

"Do you mean at work?" asked Mrs. Thorne. Her husband nodded. "But I don't understand. You're a vice president. You're certainly a part of the show when you're in charge of it."

"Any talking head can go to meetings, which is what I do all day," said Mr. Thorne. "I don't make any difference, personally."

"But don't you make decisions? Work out plans and proposals, that sort of thing?"

Mr. Thorne shrugged. *"They* do—I don't. I don't think I've had enough experience to be giving orders."

Mrs. Thorne observed, "You probably wouldn't feel very much at home here, either, if you just stood on the bank of the stream and watched the water flow by."

"She's telling you to jump right in," said Hilary seriously.

Mr. Thorne shouted with laughter, and Hilary and her mother joined him. The hills around them echoed the sound and made it last for a very long time.

"Oh, Hilary," said Mr. Thorne at last. "It seems as if it's been a long time since we've talked."

"It has been," said Hilary. "But now you're back. Where you belong."

Chapter Thirteen

HILARY CLOSED THE BOOK AND ROLLED OVER, SHUT-
ting her eyes against the last of the day's sunlight and
listening to the sounds that washed in on the tide of
clear air. Squirrels bickered in the tree outside her
window, and beneath them, in the yard, her mother
swept the last of the leaves into the compost heap,
singing quietly as she worked. The rake scraped hard
against the ground, but the sound of the leaves was
as soft as running water. Farther off on the hill, a
raccoon chirruped and another answered it, and
away down the road, in the last ring of sound, a car
began to grind up the long, slow incline.

The noise of the car came close and stopped. A
car door slammed, and Mrs. Thorne's voice rose in

cheerful greeting. Mr. Thorne's voice answered her; they laughed together.

Daddy came home earlier these days. He said he wanted to belong to his family, too; and besides, if he was going to be swimming he needed lifeguards.

Hilary smiled and opened her eyes. She bent over her notebook and chewed the end of her pencil thoughtfully. She really wanted that job on the school magazine; this essay was going to have to be *good*.

She wrote:

> *I want to write for the magazine because I'm comfortable with words. And, because I want to feel comfortable in school. You only feel like you really belong when you get involved.*

The aroma of apple pie baking teased her nose. "Hilary," called her father, "do you want to go to the Oktoberfest with us? Your mother's cooking class is serving dinner!"

Hilary called back, "You bet! I'll be right down!"

Author's Note

Here is a list of the books that Hilary read:

Grahame, Kenneth. *The Wind in the Willows*. New York: Charles Scribner's Sons, 1953.

Defoe, Daniel. *Robinson Crusoe*. New York: W. W. Norton & Co., 1975.

Conan Doyle, Sir Arthur. *A Study in Scarlet*. Reprinted in *The Annotated Sherlock Holmes*. Edited by William S. Baring-Gould. New York: Clarkson N. Potter, 1967.

Kipling, Rudyard. *The Jungle Book*. New York: Harper & Bros., 1894.

Shakespeare, William. *The Tempest*. *The Complete Works of William Shakespeare*. Edited by William Aldis Wright. Garden City: Doubleday & Co., 1936.

Forbes, Esther. *Johnny Tremain*. Boston: Houghton Mifflin Co., 1943.

O'Dell, Scott. *The Island of the Blue Dolphins*. New York: Houghton Mifflin Co., 1961.

Alcott, Louisa May. *Little Women*. New York: World Publishing Co., 1969.

L'Engle, Madeline. *A Wrinkle in Time*. New York: Farrar, Straus & Giroux, 1963.

Fitzhugh, Louise. *Harriet the Spy*. New York: Harper & Row, 1964.

Brontë, Charlotte. *Jane Eyre*. London: Oxford University Press, 1969.

Bulfinch, Thomas. *The Age of Chivalry*. New York: The New American Library, 1962.

Hamilton, Edith. *Mythology.* New York: The New American Library, 1969.

Konigsburg, E. L. *From the Mixed-up Files of Mrs. Basil E. Frankweiler.* New York: Atheneum Publishers, 1968.

Longfellow, Henry Wadsworth. "Paul Revere's Ride." In *The Best-Loved Poems of the American People.* Edited by Hazel Felleman. New York: Doubleday & Co., 1936.

Masefield, John. "Sea Fever." In *Poems.* New York: The Macmillan Co., 1935.

Twain, Mark. *The Adventures of Tom Sawyer.* New York: World Publishing Co., 1972.

Carroll, Lewis. *Alice in Wonderland.* New York: Grosset & Dunlap, 1985.

North, Sterling. *Rascal: A Memoir of a Better Era.* New York: E. P. Dutton & Co., 1963.